THE FORMATION OF COLLOIDS

MAXWELL PRESS

THE FORMATION OF COLLOIDS

THEODOR SVEDBERG

Winner of Nobel Prize for Chemistry

Professor of Physical Chemistry
in the University of Upsala

MAXWELL PRESS

Chennai   Trichy   New Delhi

MAXWELL PRESS

This edition has been published in india by arrangement with Carson Books, UK

ISBN 978-81-949040-6-9   Maxwell Press

MJP 945   © Publishers, 2023

Publisher :   C. Janarthanan

Publisher's Note

The legacy of a country is in its varied cultural heritage, historical literature, developments in the field of economy and science. The top nations in the world are competing in the field of science, economy and literature. This vast legacy has to be conserved and documented so that it can be bestowed to the future generation. The knowledge of this legacy is slowly getting perished in the present generation due to lack of documentation.

Keeping this in mind, the concern with retrospective acquiring of rare books has been accented recently by the burgeoning reprint industry. Maxwell Press is gratified to retrieve the rare collections with a view to bring back those books that were landmarks in their time.

In this effort, a series of rare books would be republished under the banner, "Maxwell Press". The books in the reprint series have been carefully selected for their contemporary usefulness as well as their historical importance within the intellectual. We reconstruct the book with slight enhancements made for better presentation, without affecting the contents of the original edition.

Most of the works selected for republishing covers a huge range of subjects, from history to anthropology. We believe this reprint edition will be a service to the numerous researchers and practitioners active in this fascinating field. We allow readers to experience the wonder of peering into a scholarly work of the highest order and seminal significance.

MAXWELL PRESS

PREFACE.

Owing to the rapid development of the science of colloids, it has become a rather difficult task to write a complete and modern text-book on this subject. The literature containing the primary material is very great, and grows greater every day. It seemed, therefore, worth while to try to give a survey of the chemistry and physics of colloids in the form of a series of small monographs, treating the main parts of the science separately. In this way it is possible to move more freely and select the problems to be reviewed according to their importance for the subject. Moreover, a series of monographs can easily be kept up to date by bringing out new editions of the books dealing with those parts of the subject that develop with special rapidity.

In the first monograph I mean to give a survey of the processes which cause the formation of colloids—or of heterogeneous systems with a relatively large boundary surface on the whole (disperse systems according to Wo. Ostwald)—especially with regard to the conditions that determine the degree of subdivision of the systems formed. As the formation of gels is a change of state within the disperse system, it will not be considered in this monograph, which deals with the formation of colloids from non-colloid material, but will be treated in one of the following monographs. In order to bring forth the leading ideas as clearly as possible, I have refrained from giving detailed directions for the preparation of the various colloids. Such information may be found in my book, *Herstellung kolloider Lösungen* (Dresden, 1909), or in the original papers referred to here.

My sincere thanks are due to Mr. Emil Hatschek for his kindness in reading the manuscript before it was sent to press.

THE SVEDBERG.

Upsala.

CONTENTS.

CONTENTS.

THE FORMATION OF COLLOIDS.

INTRODUCTION.

THE question of the formation of colloids will always be connected with the name of Thomas Graham. He was the first to point out the colloids as a special class of chemical systems, and he was the first of all investigators to discover a series of methods for preparing colloid solutions (1). The study of the works of earlier chemists has taught us since that among them there were some who dealt with colloid solutions and also, incidentally, expressed fairly correct opinions as to the constitution of colloids, as, for instance, Berzelius (2), Selmi (3), Faraday (4), but none of them drew the attention of the chemical world to the specific behaviour of colloids by means of systematic series of experimental investigations as Graham did.

Graham's opinion may be generally expressed thus : " Crystalloids and colloids represent two forms of existence ; they appear like different worlds of matter." A radical distinction is assumed " to exist between colloids and crystalloids in their intimate molecular constitution." A crystalloid and a colloid solution of the same substance must, according to this view, be considered to contain two allotropic modifications of the substance. Researches during the last two decades have considerably modified this point of view. That the colloid solutions are heterogeneous systems has, chiefly by the work of Linder and Picton (5), and especially by that of Zsigmondy (6), been proved beyond all doubt; and it is evident that, under suitable conditions, every kind of matter can be brought into colloid form without any change in its intra-molecular constitution. Present-day research considers the colloids and the crystalloids as two worlds, not from an intra-molecular point of view, but from an extra-molecular. The colloids are heterogeneous systems, but, owing to their fine structure and large relative or specific surface, they deviate considerably from such systems as were formerly looked upon as heterogeneous. In fact, they form a region between these and the crystalloid solutions. Wo. Ostwald has called them " the world of neglected dimensions, because of the lack of interest which until very lately caused them to be a disregarded field of study (7). In a system containing two or more phases, one of which is continuous (corresponding to the solvent of a common crystalloid solution), the continuous phase is called dispersion medium, and the non-continuous phases, one or more in number (corresponding to the dissolved substance or solute of a crystalloid solution), are called disperse phases (8). Graham introduced the term " sol " for a colloid solution. When the dispersion medium is water, we have a hydrosol ; when it is alcohol, an alcosol, etc.

Colloids or disperse systems in general may be formed in two ways, differing in principle : by condensation or by dispersion (9). In one case matter is brought together within a smaller boundary surface than before ; in the other case the matter is dispersed so that the specific surface is increased. In many cases diverse systems are formed by a combined process of condensation and dispersion. Often, on superficial observation, the process may be considered, for instance, as a dispersion, while an intimate analysis of the phenomenon shows that a condensation process is inserted so as to make such a process the direct cause of the formation of the disperse system (10). Examples of such " false dispersion processes " are met with in most forms of electric colloidation of metals. Thus, in general, the pulverization of metals by means of the electric arc must be a vaporization of metal with subsequent condensation to a disperse system. In the case of electrolytic pulverization the metal is often dissolved as a chemical compound, then reduced, and at the same time condensed, to a disperse system. If the state of the system in the period that directly precedes the formation of the disperse system be taken into consideration, the classification of the processes of formation in condensation and dispersion will evidently be clearly defined.

The condensation processes are far more numerous and common than the dispersion processes, and, in fact, it is quite obvious that this must be so. As every decrease of surface is accompanied by a liberation of energy and *vice versâ*, no negative surface tension being known, it is obvious that condensation is a spontaneous, dispersion a forced, process. Of course, the former case occurs more easily than the latter.

The primary condition for condensation is the *existence of a system of higher dispersity than the one desired.* If such a system, most often a molecular one, is to be produced from condensed material, this generally means the establishment of a forced process (*e.g.*, vaporization of compact metal in the electric arc). It is only then that the spontaneous process can begin to act (condensation of the metal gas to metal powder). The secondary condition for obtaining by condensation a disperse system with more than a merely ephemeral existence is the *breaking off or the retardation of the condensation process* after having reduced the surface of the system to a suitable extent.

The primary condition for dispersion is the *occurrence of a condensed system of a lower degree of dispersion than the one desired.* This low degree of dispersion can always be attained by means of a spontaneous process. The secondary condition for obtaining a somewhat stable disperse system is the *prevention or the retardation of the spontaneous retrogression of the dispersion process.*

One of the most important tasks when investigating the formation of disperse systems is to state the relations between the conditions of experiment and the degree of dispersion of the system formed.

A distinction must be made between the *primary degree of dispersion* (11), which exists immediately after the carrying out of the colloid-forming process, and the *secondary degree of dispersion*, which is most frequently brought about rather quickly in consequence of the aggregation of the primary particles, *i.e.*, by coagulation. Further, one has to consider the *tertiary degree of dispersion*, which is the result of a process very slow compared with the two former processes, *i.e.*, recrystallization. In case of condensation the *primary mean size of the particles* is determined by the number of condensation centres per unit mass of the material of the future disperse phase, and the *primary distribution of size of the particles* is regulated by the supply of material to the various condensation centres. If, for instance, centres are generated or inserted into the system during the condensation itself, those centres that appear later will receive less material than the earlier ones, and thus they will become smaller than these (12).

The centres of condensation may :

1. *Be present in the system before the condensation process sets in* or be *introduced independently of the processes that lead to condensation* (*e.g.*, condensation of vapour on ions in the adiabatic expansion experi-

ments of C. T. R. Wilson (13), precipitation of gold on small gold particles according to Zsigmondy (14)).

2. Or they may be *formed by the condensation process or in intimate connection with it* (e.g., ordinary reduction of gold to gold colloid).

Case 1 is of course by far the more simple and the more easily controlled. Besides the number of centres and the transport of mass to them, *i.e.*, time of condensation for every single centre, one has to take into account the nature of the centres or nuclei. It has been shown that some nuclei are able to cause condensation at high degrees of supersaturation but not at low ones, while other kinds of nuclei extend their action to lower degrees of supersaturation. In such a case the degree of dispersion rises with the supersaturation.

In case 2, where the nuclei are formed exclusively or to a great extent by the condensation process, it is necessary to know how they are formed in order to estimate the relation between the experimental conditions and the degree of dispersion. In this respect our knowledge is still very incomplete. It seems that the primary degree of dispersion always rises with the supersaturation, and consequently in general with concentration (15). If, however, the process by which the material for the condensation is produced does not take place fast enough, it may happen that the supersaturation does not rise but falls with the concentration (16). In many cases where a fall of the degree of dispersion occurs with increasing concentration it may be due to the fact that it is not the primary but the secondary, or even the tertiary, degree of dispersion that is observed.

BIBLIOGRAPHY.

1. Graham, *Phil. Trans.*, 151, 183 (1861).
2. Berzelius, *Lehrb. d. Chem.*, 3 Aufl., 3, 65 (1834) ; 5 Aufl., 2, 269 (1844).

3. Selmi, *Nuovi Ann. di Scienze Natur.*, Bologna (2), **8**, 404 (1847). *Cf. Koll.-Zeitschr.*, **8**, 113 (1911).

4. Faraday, *Phil. Trans.*, **147**, 145 (1857).

5. Linder and Picton, *Journ. Chem. Soc.*, **61**, 114, 137 and 148 (1892) ; **67**, 63 (1895).

6. Zsigmondy, *Zur Erkenntnis der Kolloide*, Jena (1905).

7. Wo. Ostwald, *Die Welt der vernachlässigten Dimensionen*, Dresden (1915).

8. Wo. Ostwald, *Koll.-Zeitschr.*, **1**, 291 (1907).

9. Svedberg, *Nova acta*, Upsala (4), **2**, No. 1, p. 3 (1907).

10. Svedberg, *Herstellung kolloider Lösungen*, Dresden, p. 1 (1909). Kohlschütter, *Die Erscheinungsformen der Materie*, Leipzig, p. 180 (1917).

11. *Cf.* Mecklenburg, *Zeitschr. anorg. Chem.*, **74**, 262 (1912). Odén, *Arkiv för kemi.*, Stockholm, **7**, No. 26, p. 4 (1920).

12. Zsigmondy, *Kolloidchemie*, 2te Aufl., Leipzig, p. 144 (1918).

13. C. T. R. Wilson, *Phil. Trans.*, **A189**, 265 (1897) ; **A192**, 403 (1899).

14. Zsigmondy, *Zeitschr. phys. Chem.*, **56**, 65 (1906).

15. v. Weimarn, *Grundzüge der Dispersoidchemie*, Dresden, p. 54 (1911) ; *Zur Lehre von den Zuständen der Materie*, Dresden, p. 165 (1914). Odén, *Arkiv för kemi.*, Stockholm, **7**, No. 26, p. 33 (1920).

16. Picton, *Journ. Chem. Soc.*, **61**, 137 (1892). Biltz, *Nachr. Ges. Wiss.*, Göttingen, Math.-Phys. Klasse, 1906, p. 141. Svedberg, *Zeitschr. phys. Chem.*, **65**, 624 (1909).

FORMATION OF DISPERSE SYSTEMS
IN VACUO.

THE simplest form of *condensation* is the one that takes place *in vacuo* (1).   Here we have no ordinary dispersion medium, and the disperse system formed can exist only through the support of a solid or fluid surface, which acts as a dispersion medium.   The origin and nature of such condensates are of considerable interest in judging of the primary qualities of condensation.   The researches of M. Knudsen (2) and L. Hamburger (3) have shown that the condensation *in vacuo* is determined to a great extent by the temperature of the walls and of the gas just before condensation takes place.   According to Knudsen, it seems that a metal molecule which encounters a surface of the same substance always adheres to it.   If the surface consists of another material there is a critical temperature dividing the domain of temperature into two parts.   Below this point the molecule adheres to the surface, above it the molecule is reflected.   For a glass wall and mercury molecules Knudsen found the critical temperature to be about $-135°$, for glass and silver it is above $+575°$.   Thus mercury vapour adheres without reflection to a glass surface colder than $-135°$, and silver when it is colder than $+575°$.   The consequence of the absence of reflection is that if an object is placed between the source of the metal gas and the wall a shadow free from condensate will be seen on it.   The metal molecules are (*in vacuo*) sent out in straight lines from the source (*e.g.,* from a fine incandescent wire), and in the case of non-reflection the part of the wall that lies in shadow will get no condensate on it. Above the critical point there is no shadow, for metal is brought over to the shaded part of the wall by diffuse reflection. On account of the complete reflection of the metal vapour by a glass wall of a temperature above the critical point, very high degrees of supersaturation may be obtained. R. Wood (4) and L. Hamburger have observed this phenomenon in cadmium. Thus Hamburger found that a cadmium wire heated *in vacuo* by means of an electric current gave off gas that did not condense on a glass wall at ordinary temperatures. If the wall was touched with a cotton plug dipped in liquid air, a rapid condensation took place at that very point and lasted even when the cooling had been stopped. Magnesium and zinc showed the same phenomenon, but it was never observed with silver, gold, platinum, tungsten, molybdenum, nickel, iron and copper. These metals are distinguished by the shadow phenomenon. According to Knudsen, the critical condensation temperature lies below $-78°$ for cadmium, magnesium and zinc. It seems that condensates formed on a wall cooled below the critical point have a much higher degree of dispersion than those formed above it. It also appears that even within the region above it a lower temperature of the wall gives to the condensate a higher degree of dispersion. The temperature of the metal gas is also a very important factor. Thus Hamburger has shown that elements with a very high melting point, such as tungsten, carbon, molybdenum, platinum, nickel, iron, give condensates of a very high degree of dispersion, often optically quite unresolvable and without any Tyndall light. In his experiments these elements, owing to their high melting points, could be brought to very high temperatures. Such elements as silver, gold, copper, which could not be heated to those very high temperatures, gave condensates of a little lower degree of dispersion, and the easily melted metals, magnesium, zinc, cadmium, gave the coarsest condensates. Thus it is obvious that *the degree of dispersion rises with the difference of temperature between the metal gas and the wall, viz., with the degree of supersaturation.*

In these condensation experiments we are dealing with the highest differences of temperature that can possibly be obtained. Thus, for instance, the difference in temperature between tungsten gas from an incandescent tungsten wire and a cold wall is about 3,000°. Hamburger's ultra-microscopic investigations of the condensates and his measurements of their electric conductivity, carried out in collaboration with E. Osterhuis, prove that some of these condensates, especially those derived from very high melting metals and condensed at low temperatures, are to be looked upon as real films of amorphous metal. These films disintegrate in time spontaneously int discrete particles, probably with crystallization. Heating accelerates the disintegration, and it seems that the higher the vapour pressure of the metal, the easier the disintegration of the film. Tungsten, which of all substances has the lowest vapour pressure, gives the most stable films (thickness down to $0 \cdot 5 \mu\mu$) ; silver, with a considerably higher vapour pressure, gives very unstable films; while cadmium, zinc and magnesium, with their high vapour pressure, give no films at all, but only granular condensates, the degree of dispersity of which is lowered rather rapidly in consequence of the growth of the larger grains at the expense of the smaller ones. This disintegration of the continuous metal films into particles is to be considered as a continued condensation, for the surface of the new system is no doubt smaller than that of the film.

In transferring the condensates thus formed into

the liquid state a considerable decrease in the degree of dispersion takes place. Thus Knudsen observed that continuous films of mercury, brown in transmitted light, which had been formed at a low temperature ($-183°$), disintegrated into small drops when the temperature was allowed to rise.

If the glass wall on which condensation is to take place is covered beforehand with a thin film (for example, 10 $\mu\mu$ thick) of some salt, no coherent metal film is formed. Probably the metal molecules are separated by the salt molecules. Such films represent in a fresh condition, and at low metal content, a sort of solid solution of metal in salt, and, when old and with higher metal content, probably a very fine-grained metal colloid, the salt acting as a dispersion medium. They have a considerably lower light absorption than the coherent metal films or the fine-grained pure condensates of metal particles. In order to prevent the darkening of electric incandescent lamps, the makers have recently begun to cover the inside of the glass globes with very thin films of certain salts, and the result has been very good indeed. These observations are of great value for our opinion as to the formation of disperse systems in the solid state, which will be explained in detail, below.

No *dispersion* processes taking place *in vacuo* have as yet been studied.

BIBLIOGRAPHY.

1. M. L. Houllevigue, *Ann. chim. et phys.* (8), **20**, 138 (1910).
2. M. Knudsen, *Annal. Phys.* (4), **50**, 472 (1916).
3. L. Hamburger, *Koll.-Zeitschr.*, **23**, 177 (1918).
4. R. Wood, *Phil. Mag.* (6), **32**, 364 (1916).

FORMATION OF DISPERSE SYSTEMS IN GASES—THE GASEOUS DISPERSION MEDIUM IN SOME CASES SUBSEQUENTLY EXCHANGED FOR A LIQUID ONE.

NEXT to condensation *in vacuo*, the simplest case we have to consider is condensation in an indifferent gas. It appears that the nature of the gas has a considerable influence on the degree of dispersion of the condensate. Two investigations of V. Kohlschütter, one dealing with the vaporization of metals by heat in a glass or quartz tube and condensation on a glass wall (I), and the other vaporization of metals by means of canal rays and condensation on a glass wall (= cathodic disintegration *in vacuo*) (2), are of great interest. In both cases *the degree of dispersion of the condensate rises with the molecular weight of the indifferent gas* (Fig. I). Thus cadmium and zinc gave more finely grained condensates in nitrogen than in hydrogen, arsenic and selenium more finely grained ones in carbon dioxide than in hydrogen. When silver is vaporized by canal rays the condensate is most fine-grained in argon, less so in nitrogen, and çoarsest in hydrogen. This relation between the molecular weight and the degree of dispersion of the system formed vanishes with increasing rarefaction of the gas. It is, however, perceptible at rather low pressures, and is still marked at 50 mm. Kohlschütter found that *the degree of dispersion of the condensate rises with the pressure of the gas* (Fig. I). This appears to be opposed to Hamburger's observation of very highly disperse metal condensates *in vacuo*. When

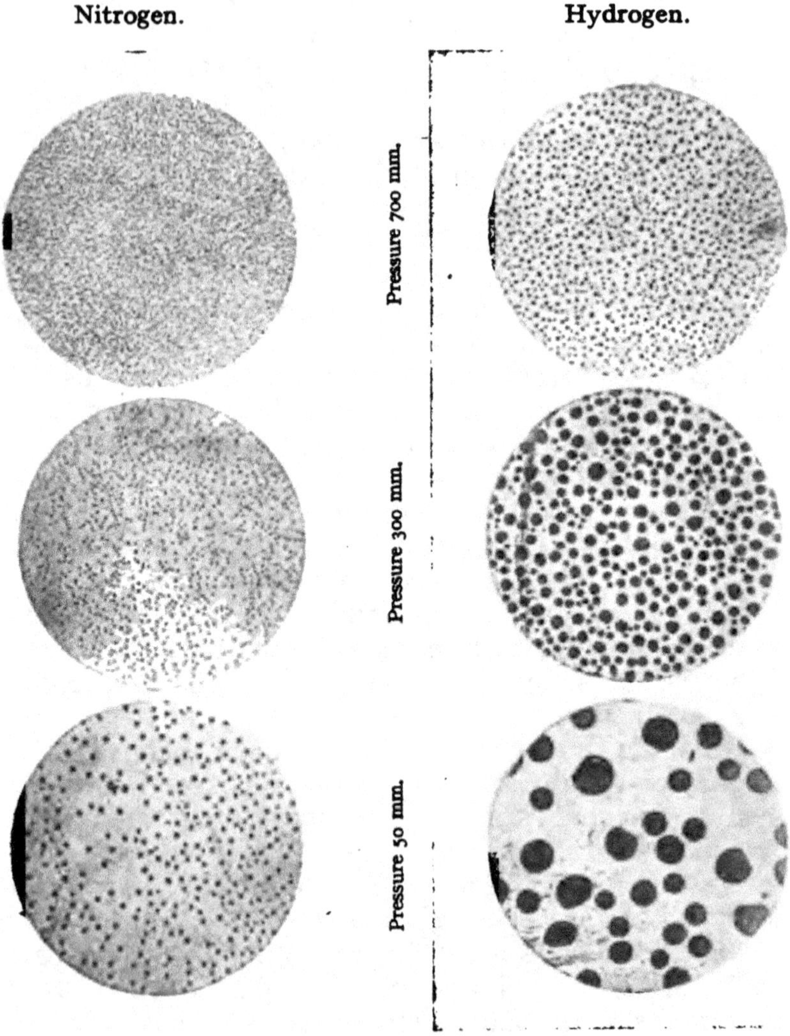

Nitrogen.   Hydrogen.

Pressure 700 mm.

Pressure 300 mm.

Pressure 50 mm.

FIG. 1.—Condensation of zinc vapours.   (According to Kohlschütter.)

collecting the condensate on a wall in the presence of a gas, the condensation probably takes place to some extent in the gas itself, *i.e.*, *near* the wall, but not *on* the wall. *In vacuo* the condensation must, of course, take place *on* the wall. This may account for the above-mentioned discrepancy between the observations of Kohlschütter and Hamburger.

By the injection of superheated mercury vapour into water I. Nordlund prepared disperse systems of mercury (3). The degree of dispersion was rather high in part of the system. Here we are obviously concerned with the condensation of mercury vapour in an atmosphere of water vapour. The condensation may partly take place more freely in this atmosphere, partly close to the cool water-surface. The small mercury droplets seem to be formed in the latter, the large ones in the former way.

Some very peculiar observations made by Kimura (4) would have come under this heading had they been correct. Kimura heated a metal wire (in a flame or by means of an electric current) and dipped it quickly in water. An ultra-microscopic examination proved the presence of some small particles. In the case of the easily oxidizable metals, aluminium, zinc, iron, nickel, antimony, tin, bismuth, Kimura's observations are to be explained by the action of an oxidation process. In the case of platinum and gold the explanation might have been as follows : The incandescent wire is to some extent surrounded by a layer of metal vapour, and by immersing the wire in water this vapour is condensed in an atmosphere of water vapour to ultra-microscopic particles, which are then taken up by the water. A careful examination of Kimura's experiments by H. Nordenson (5) has proved, however, that in the case of platinum and gold no formation of metallic particles takes place. The particles observed by Kimura are to be explained as dust or some other contamination brought into the water during the process.

The most effective method for the vaporization of the metals is to form an electric arc between electrodes of the metal in question. Even the most refractory metals are in this way vaporized rather abundantly. The amount of vaporization and the degree of dispersion of the colloid formed depend not only on the electric properties of the arc (*i.e.*, potential difference, current intensity, and period of current), but also on the nature of the surrounding gases and the solid or liquid surfaces near to it. It has been customary to distinguish between arc dispersion in gases and in liquids. In both cases, however, the arc is burning in gas; the difference lies only in the manner of condensation of the metal vapour. Even in this respect there are transition forms, and thus it seems most rational to treat all these phenomena together and to consider them all under the heading "Formation of Disperse Systems in Gases."

With regard to the electrical conditions, there are two extreme cases: direct current arc and high-frequency current arc. Transition forms between these are, intermittent current arc and low-frequency alternating current arc. From a thermal point of view there are two forms to be considered, free arc and enclosed arc. With regard to condensation, we have condensation in gas, on a liquid surface, and on a solid surface.

If a direct current arc, for instance, between silver electrodes, is maintained in an indifferent gas, *e.g.*, nitrogen, the condensation takes place in the nitrogen, and a rather coarse condensate is produced, settling gradually on the solid walls of the vessel. But, as F. Ehrenhaft and his students have shown, the smallest particles remain suspended in the gas for hours (6). According to some incidental observations made by these investigators the degree of dispersion rises as the strength of the current diminishes (7).

If the arc is permitted to burn close to a solid

surface—for instance, of glass—in such a way that the hot metal gas strikes the surface, part of the metal gas is condensed on it. Owing to the rapid cooling, and probably, also, to the breaking off of the coagulation process, the degree of dispersion of this condensate is higher than when it is formed freely in the gas. If the arc is allowed to burn close above the surface of a liquid, the condensation takes place partly in the surface, and this condensate is taken up by the liquid, forming a colloid solution (8). The degree of dispersion is greater than when the condensation takes place in a gas.

The condensation on a liquid surface can be brought to completion by surrounding the arc on all sides with liquid. Thus we have the submerged arc or the so-called arc pulverization process in a liquid. It seems, however, that, even in this case, the main part of the metal gas is condensed in the vapour from the liquid that surrounds the arc, and not on the surface between the vapour and the liquid. The metal vaporization in the arc is much greater if the arc is surrounded by a liquid than by a gas. Thus the loss in weight of the electrodes in the case of the cadmium arc of 1·0 ampere is, in nitrogen, about 0·0004 gm. per minute ; in ethyl ether, 0·0016 gm. per minute, or four times more in ether than in nitrogen (8). The explanation of this increased vaporization of metal may be as follows : Owing to the effective condensation the equilibrium in the arc is rapidly disturbed, and this causes abundant vaporization of metal in order to re-establish the equilibrium.

Besides the metal gas and the gaseous products from the surrounding liquid, the arc also contains metal globules formed from the melted metal on the electrode surfaces by the action of electro-mechanical forces. Some of these melting globules leave the arc and are taken up by the surrounding liquid, forming a rather coarse sediment on the bottom of the vessel (9).

The portion of the colloid formed by condensation of metal gas has a much higher degree of dispersion than the portion formed by dispersion of melted metal from the electrodes. The loss in weight of the electrodes rises proportionally to the square of the current, and is but little influenced by the length of the arc. The decomposition of the medium by the

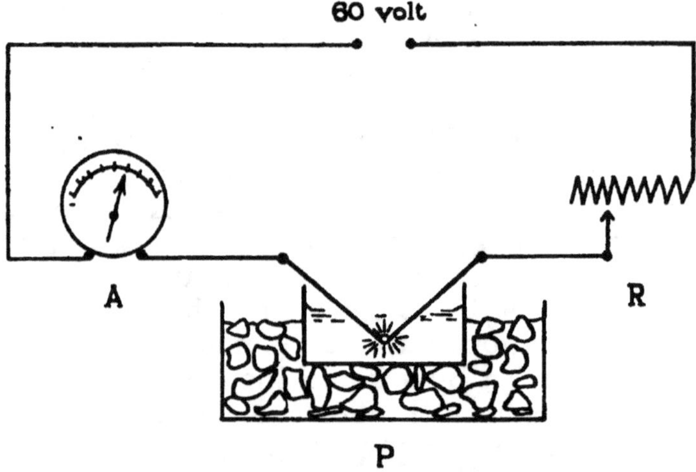

FIG. 2.—Arrangement of electric pulverization.
(According to Bredig.)

arc increases very rapidly as the length of the arc increases (10).

The preparation of colloid solutions by means of the arc was discovered y Bredig (1898) (11), and has since been studied specially by the writer and his collaborators (1907–1920) (12). Bredig used a continuous current of 5 to 10 amperes and 30 to 110 volts, and the arc was allowed to burn freely in the liquid. As a dispersion medium he used pure water that was cooled by immersing in ice and water the vessel in which the arc was burning. Fig. 2 gives the arrangement for electric pulverization according to Bredig. A is an ammeter, P the pulverization vessel, and R an adjustable resistance.

He obtained hydrosols of the noble metals, viz., platinum, palladium, iridium, gold, and silver. Using very pure, cooled water that had been freed from air, he could even get the hydrosol of cad-mium. More positive metals than cadmium give sols of their oxides. Degen (1902) (13) and Burton (1906) (14) tried to disperse metals in organic liquids, such as ethyl alcohol and methyl alcohol, by means of the arc, but the considerable decomposition of the medium prevented the formation of pure and stable sols.

The mean temperature of the continuous current arc, and, consequently, the vaporization of metal in it, can be considerably increased by using a suitable thermal protection. Thus we get what the writer has called an *enclosed arc* in contradistinction to the free arc described above. It has been shown that of the two.electrodes the anode is most sensitive to thermal protection. Of course, this phenomenon is the more marked the greater the cooling power of the surrounding medium. Thus it is more marked when the arc is immersed in a liquid than in a gas. If an arc between silver wires of about 1 mm. diameter is enclosed in a quartz tube provided with a little hole right in front of the arc, and if a current of nitrogen is let in from both ends of the tube, as shown in Fig. 3, we get an effective arrangement for producing silver vapour of high temperature and great concentration. A magnetic field may be applied in order to facilitate the emergence of the silver gas through the hole.

If there is a great distance between the hole of the quartz tube from which the nitrogen gas loaded with silver vapour emerges and any solid or fluid wall, the result is a condensate, the degree of dispersion of which is equal to the condensate obtained from the free arc in a gas.   If, however, the aforesaid distance is small enough to let the silver vapour, while

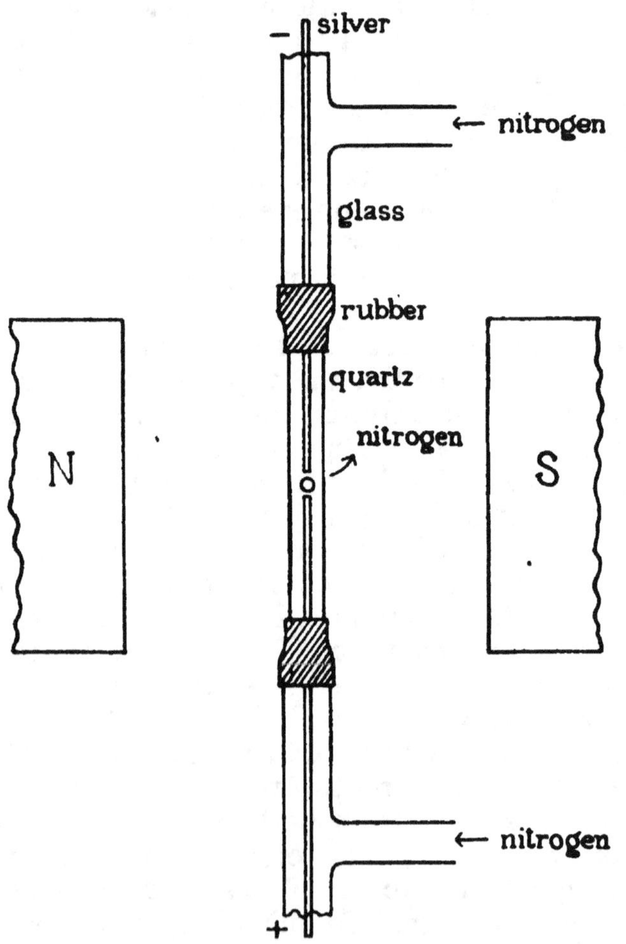

FIG. 3.—Arrangement for the production of silver vapour.

still hot, encounter a solid or fluid wall, a condensate with a much higher degree of dispersion is formed. Thus we get a highly disperse, yellowish-red condensate on a glass wall placed some millimetres in front of the hole, while the free arc only produces a black, coarse condensate. If the arc vapours are blown against an ethyl alcohol surface, the silver vapour is condensed to very small particles, which form a reddish-yellow alcosol. The free silver arc burning close to an alcohol surface also produces a silver alcosol, though a rather dilute one, and the particles are much greater, the sol being greenish-black in

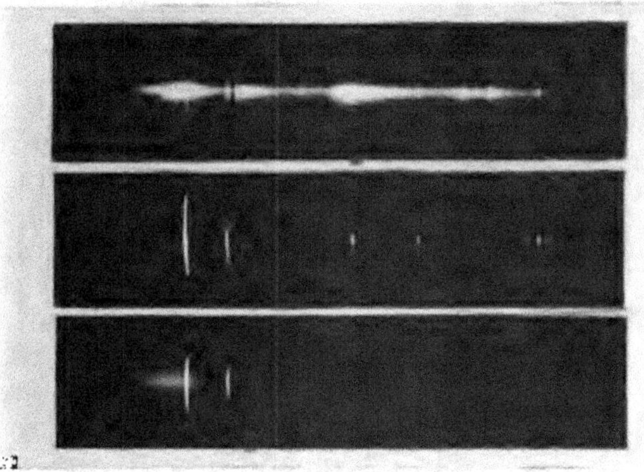

Fig. 4.—Spectrum of the free silver arc in ethyl alcohol (*a*) ; the free silver arc in nitrogen (*b*) ; and the enclosed silver arc in ethyl alcohol (*c*).

colour. Thus the higher the speed of the condensation process and the shorter the period during which the particles are kept in the gaseous medium (where coagulation proceeds very rapidly), the higher the degree of dispersion of the product formed.

If the hole in the quartz tube opens *under* the surface of a liquid, the condensation and, consequently, also the formation of colloid, are much more complete. In some experiments with the quartz tube immersed in ethyl alcohol the writer found a formation of colloid several times greater than with the free arc immersed in the same liquid. When hot metal vapour condenses on a liquid surface there is the risk that some chemical decomposition of the liquid may take place. This process is still more marked if the liquid is allowed to touch the hot electrodes, and if vapours of the liquid get into the arc. Spectroscopical investigations have shown that in the case of the free arc, *e.g.*, silver in ethyl alcohol, the arc is to some extent built up of gas from the liquid. This gas is partly decomposed, the spectrum of the arc showing, in addition to the silver lines, the band spectrum of carbon (Fig. 4, *a*). The spectrum of the free silver arc in nitrogen is given in Fig. 4, *b*.

In the case of the enclosed arc (arrangement shown by Fig. 5), however, the hot nitrogen and silver gases coming out from the hole in the quartz tube and encountering the alcohol only cause very slight decomposition, the spectrum of the arc showing only the silver lines and some continuous light probably emitted by the hot quartz tube (Fig. 4, *c*).

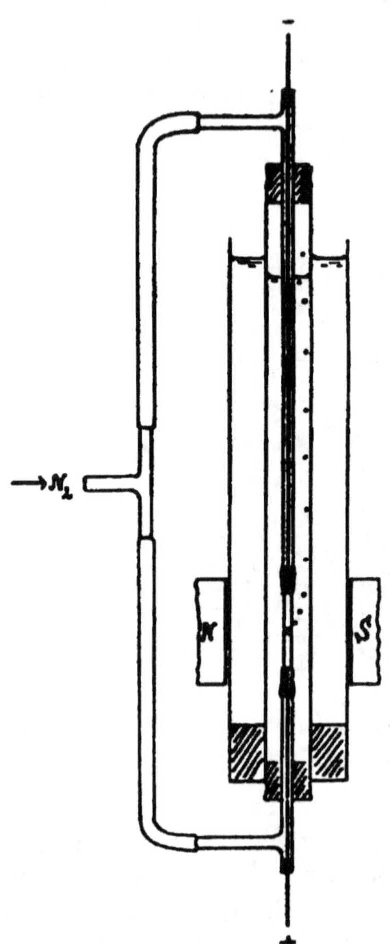

Fig. 54. — Arrangement for electric pulverization of metals with enclosed arc.

It is obvious that the glowing parts of the quartz
tube are emitting vapours of silicic acid, and, as a

Fig. 5b.—Apparatus for electric pulverization of metals
with enclosed arc.

matter of fact, the colloids formed contain considerable amounts of colloid silicic acid.   In a silver
alcosol prepared by means of this arrangement

Börjeson found the disperse phase to contain 40 per cent. of silicic acid.

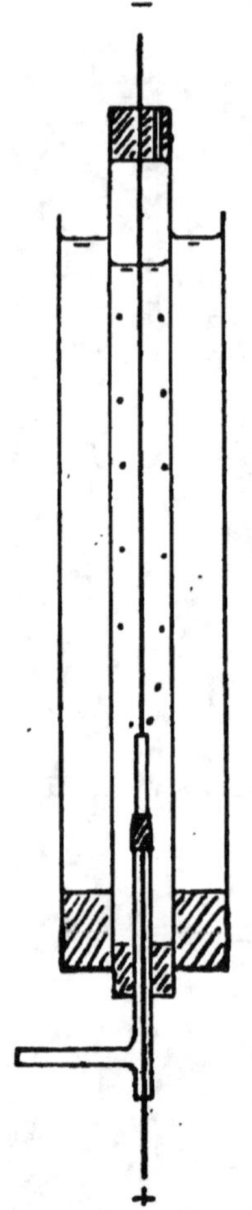

FIG. 6.—Arrangement for electric pulverization of metals with partly protected arc.

As stated above, a considerable change takes place in the production of colloid, even when only the anode, and not the cathode, is thermally protected against the cooling power of the liquid. Thus with the arrangement indicated by Fig. 6 we get a silver colloid of a much higher degree of dispersion than with the free silver arc in alcohol.

The nature of the indifferent gas used in the experiments with the enclosed arc influences the degree of dispersion of the system formed. Thus in the case of the only partly protected arc (Fig. 6) we get a coarser colloid when using hydrogen instead of nitrogen as the indifferent gas. In the case of the completely enclosed arc (Fig. 5) the difference is only slight. It is of interest to notice that Kohlschütter observed just the same difference between nitrogen and hydrogen with regard to the condensation on a glass wall of metal vapour produced in a purely thermal way. The agreement may, perhaps, be only accidental ; as far as the arc is concerned, the phenomenon can be explained by the greater thermal conductivity, i.e., the greater cooling power of the hydrogen, while in Kohlschütter's experiment the explanation can hardly be the one suggested.

The intermittent current arc, such as we get it, for instance, by inserting a mercury turbine interrupter (interruption number about 150 per second) in the current circuit of a common direct current arc, differs from the ordinary continuous arc in the following respect (15) : the portion of the system formed that consists of rather large particles is much increased.   This is just what might be expected, for

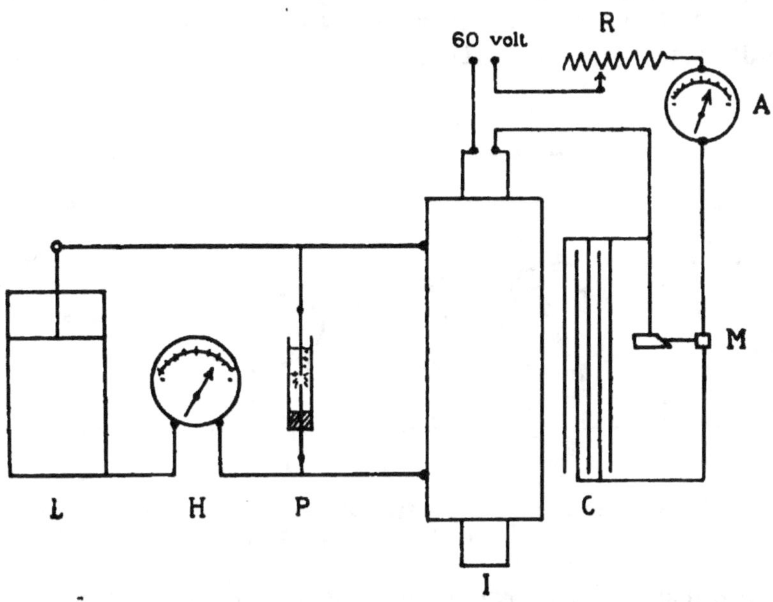

FIG. 7.—Arrangement for electric pulverization of metals with damped oscillating arc.

in the case of the intermittent arc the metal gas as well as the vapours from the liquid are condensed to a great extent, or even completely, at every interruption, thus causing the liquid to fill up the space formerly occupied by the arc and scattering the melting globules of arc into the surrounding liquid.   The low-frequency alternating current arc (frequency about 50 per second) produces nearly the same kind of disperse systems as the intermittent arc.

The arc formed by an alternating current of very high frequency—a so-called oscillatory current—(period 10^{-7} to 10^{-4} seconds) shows a rather different behaviour. Two forms of such arcs have been studied, viz., the damped oscillatory arc produced by a Leyden jar circuit (16) and the undamped oscillatory arc (wave current) (17) as produced by a sort of Poulsen circuit invented by the writer (18). Figs. 7 and 8 show the arrangement of apparatus. L is a Leyden jar, H a hot-wire ammeter, P the pulverization apparatus, I an induction coil, C a

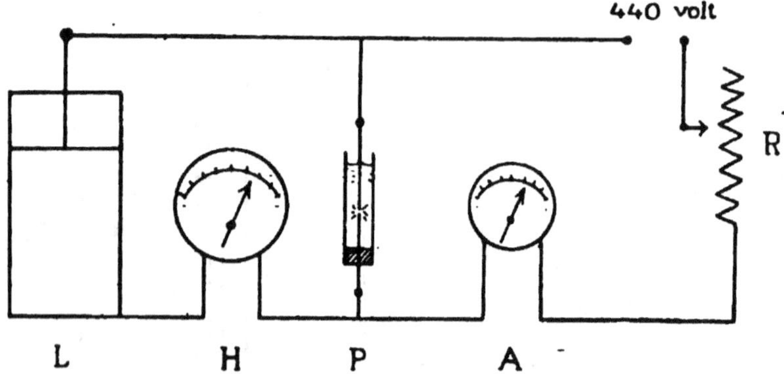

FIG. 8.—Arrangement for electric pulverization of metals with undamped oscillating arc.

condenser, M a mercury interrupter, R an adjustable resistance, A an ordinary ammeter.

We will first consider the oscillatory arc with damping. If the arc is surrounded by a gas, the loss in weight of the electrodes, *i.e.*, the production of colloid, is very small, only about $\frac{1}{10}$ of the value observed for the free direct current arc, the effective intensity of the current being the same. If, however, the arc is immersed in a liquid, the loss of weight is of the same order of magnitude as for the free continuous current arc in a liquid. Just as in the case of the low-frequency alternating current arc and the intermittent current arc two different processes take place, viz., vaporization of the metal and condensation of the metal gas to small particles and a real dispersion of melted metal (19). The dispersion product formed is separated by a rather large interval from the part of the disperse phase formed by the condensation process, and it can easily be removed from the condensate by means of sedimentation. In the case of cadmium in ethyl alcohol the radius of the globules formed by pure dispersion lies between the limits 0·5 to 25 μ, while the mean value of the radius of the condensation product is about 5 $\mu\mu$. For tin the average maximum value of the radius was found to be about 10 μ and for bismuth 100 μ. These figures, of course, only indicate the order of magnitude of the radii.

When pulverizing electrodes of a binary alloy in ethyl alcohol Börjeson found that the two metals were distributed between the condensation and the dispersion products in the following way. If the two metals had nearly the same boiling point the sediment and the disperse phase of the colloid solution were found to have about the same composition. If the metals had different boiling points the sediment was richer in the metal of high boiling point (Table 1). This statement is strong evidence in favour of the view that the sol is formed by condensation of metal gas and the sediment by dispersion of melted metal. As to the composition of the various parts of the sediment, it was found that the fine-grained fractions contained less of the volatile metal than did the coarser fractions. This fact shows that the melting globules must have been formed when the arc was still burning and that they must have remained in the arc for some time, permitting the volatile metal to evaporate to some extent from the surface of the globules. Owing to their larger specific surface the evaporation per unit mass must, of course, be greater in the case of the smaller globules than in the case of the larger ones. The hypothesis suggested by Benedicks (20) that the melting globules are formed by the streaming of the liquid against the molten parts of the electrode surfaces when the arc breaks down at the interruptions of the current cannot be supported. If such a process occurs it must be of very little importance.

TABLE I.

Alloy and boiling point of components.	In electrodes.	In sediment.		In sol.
		Coarse fraction.	Fine-grained fraction.	
Au (2,500°)—Cd (780°)	0·84	1·7	3·0	0·52
Au (2,500°)—Sn (2,270°)	0·74	0·75	0·81	0·71
Bi (1,420°)—Cd (780°)	1·0	1·4	2·0	0·77

In liquids the high-frequency arc always produces more finely grained and purer colloids than the free continuous or low-frequency arc. The amount of condensate and of dispersion product and their degrees of dispersion as well as the decomposition of the liquid (the dispersion medium) depend on the electrical conditions of the oscillation circuit, viz., intensity of current, capacity, self-induction, resistance, length of the arc, etc. They are also dependent on the nature of the electrode metal and the nature and temperature of the dispersion medium.

With a capacity of about 0·0004 m.f., low self-induction and low resistance in the oscillation circuit, the fraction of the disperse phase produced by pure dispersion is about 20 per cent. for cadmium in ethyl alcohol. With increasing capacity this fraction increases, amounting to about 40 per cent. at a capacity of 0·003 m.f. and to about 55 per cent. at 0·09 m.f. In the case of metals with a high melting point the fraction produced by pure dispersion is smaller than in the case of a metal of low melting point (Table 2) (21).

TABLE 2.

Medium = ethyl alcohol. Capacity = 0·003 m.f.
Current intensity = 1·4 to 1·7 amperes.

Metal.	Dispersion product in percentage of total loss in weight of electrodes.	Melting point.
Pt	20·2	1,700°
Au	25·8	1,064°
Zn	41·0	419°
Cd	41·6	320°
Sn	56·8	232°
Bi	59·3	268°

The loss in weight of the electrodes is proportional to the square of the virtual current and is equal for both electrodes. In Fig. 9 the curves representing the relation between current and total loss in weight of electrodes in ethyl ether are shown.

The current intensity being equal, the pulverization decreases a little with increasing capacity, increases a little with increasing self-induction, decreases rapidly with increased resistance and with increased arc length. The decomposition of the medium decreases rapidly with increased capacity, and increases rapidly with increased self-induction, increased resistance, and a little with increased arc length. Low temperature depresses the decomposition of the medium considerably, but has no perceptible influence on the rate of pulverization of the

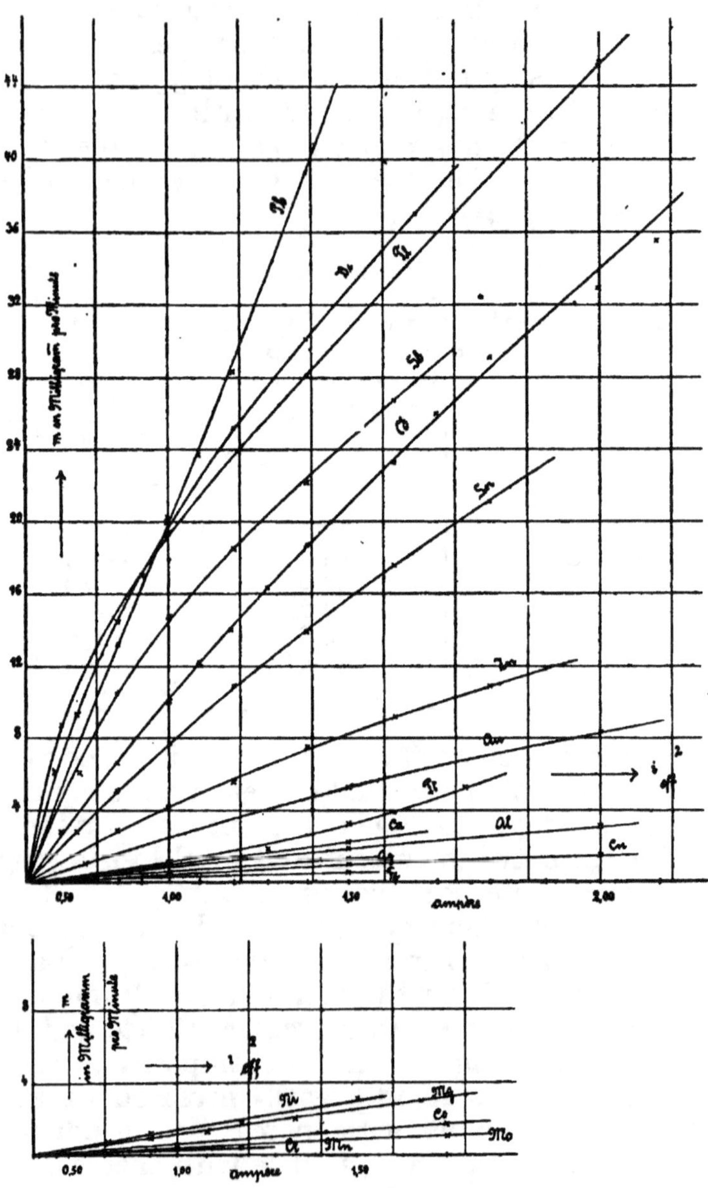

FIG. 9.—Variation of total loss in weight of electrodes per
minute with current in the case of electric pulverization
in ethyl ether by means of the damped oscillatory arc.

electrodes. Hence the ratio between decomposition of medium and pulverization of electrodes is smallest when the capacity is great, when the self-induction, the resistance and the arc length are small, and when the temperature is low. Under these circumstances we also get the purest sols.

The question of the relation between the degree of dispersion of the condensate and the experimental conditions is a rather complicated one. Coagulation sets in immediately after the formation of the particles, and .thus alters the degree of dispersion in a manner very difficult to control. Börjeson by measuring .the decrease of the degree of dispersion with time was able to calculate the approximate size of the particles at the time zero, and found the initial degree of dispersion to be almost independent of capacity, self-induction, and current intensity. The initial size of particles was found to be larger in fluids of higher viscosity and accordingly somewhat larger at low temperatures. The particles from various metals do not generally differ much in size. About one minute after the formation of the sol Börjeson found the following figures (Table 3) :—

TABLE 3.

Oscillatory arc. Medium : ethyl alcohol.
Temperature $= - 75°$.

Metal.	Radius of particles in $\mu\mu$.
Au	2·8
Zn	2·9
Pt	3·8
Cd	5·0
Sn	12·6
Bi	17

The large values of Sn and Bi may be due to coagulation.

The decrease in the degree of dispersion in most cases reached a limiting value after some time, and this secondary degree of dispersion was found to depend on many factors. Low temperature is · one of the principal means for attaining sols of high secondary degree of dispersion. Further, the rate of production of colloid must be slow, *i.e.*, the capacity and the intensity of current must not be too high and the arc not too short.

By means of this form of electric pulverization the sols of almost all metals have been obtained (22). The following dispersion media have been used : water; methyl, ethyl, propyl, butyl, and amyl alcohol; ethyl ether; acetone; ethyl and amyl acetate; chloroform, etc. As pulverization apparatus the writer used a kind of spark-micrometer that could be immersed into a beaker filled with dispersion medium (Fig. 10). In preparing the sols of the alkali metals it is necessary to work in an indifferent atmosphere and to use an indifferent

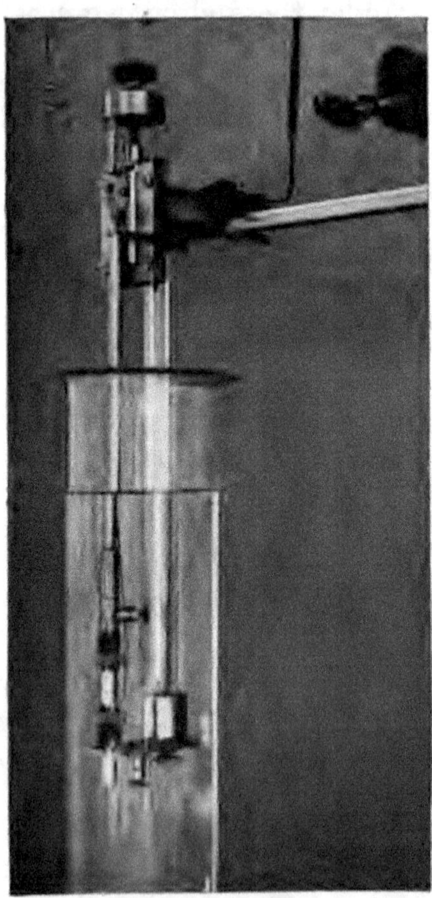

Fig. 10.—Spark micrometer for electric pulverization of metals.

dispersion medium, *e.g.*, ethyl ether, of a high degree of purity.   Low temperature facilitates the process.   In Fig. 11 a suitable apparatus for the preparation of sodium and potassium sols is represented. Some fragments of the metal to be pulverized are introduced into the tube T, which is provided with two holes at the bottom and two platinum wire electrodes P_1 and P_2.   The flask F contains a supply of dispersion medium and some purifying substance, *e.g.*, sodium wire in the case of ethyl ether.   Hydrogen can be conducted through T and F by means of the rubber tubes R_1 and R_2. Sparking and pulverization go on almost automatically when the current is closed, and can be facilitated by slightly tapping the tube T.

With regard to the production of colloids by means of the high-frequency arc without damping (" wave current arc "), the process on the whole very much resembles that with the damped high-frequency arc.

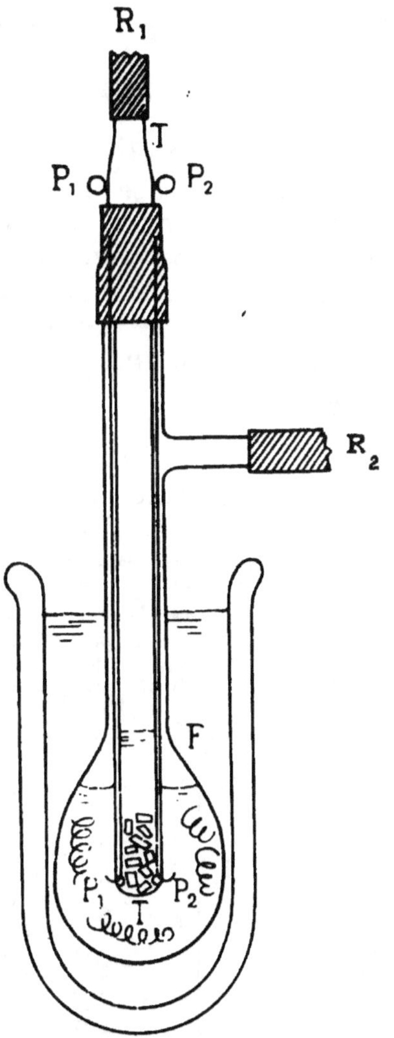

FIG. 11. — Apparatus for the preparation of sodium and potassium sols.

It differs from it in the following respect : The production of colloid is much greater in the case of the wave current arc. For 1 ampere it is about three times as great. The decomposition for 1 ampere is, however, only increased to about double, so that the specific decomposition, *i.e.*, the ratio between decomposition and loss in weight of electrodes, is smaller in the case of the wave current arc. The order of the various metals, arranged according to the total loss in weight of electrodes per minute, is not quite the same in the case of the wave current as in that of the damped oscillatory current arc. In Table 4 some figures demonstrating this fact are given.

TABLE 4.

Current intensity $= 1\cdot5$ ampere.

Oscillatory current arc; capacity $= 0\cdot003$ m.f.		Wave current arc; capacity $= 0\cdot013$ m.f.	
Metal.	Total loss in weight of electrodes in milligrammes per minute.	Metal.	Total loss in weight of electrodes in milligrammes per minute.
Pb . .	45	Sb . .	130
Bi . .	33	Bi . .	75
Sb . .	25	Pb . .	64
Cd . .	21	Cd . .	48
Zn . .	8	Zn . .	25
Au . .	6	Au . .	10
Pt . .	3	Pt . .	4
Al . .	2	Ag . .	2·6
Ag . .	1·3	Cu . .	2·0
Cu . .	1·0	Al . .	0·1

The loss in weight of electrodes is not equally divided between cathode and anode, but the anode loses more than the cathode. With increasing length of arc this difference becomes less marked. The ratio between dispersion and condensation product is a little less than in the case of the damped oscillatory arc. The secondary degree of dispersion of the colloid formed is about the same as in the case of the damped oscillatory arc, but macroscopic coagulation often takes place during or immediately after the formation.

Another method of preparing disperse systems with metal as disperse phase, which is clearly related to the process just described, consists in passing an electric current of high intensity through a foil or wire of the metal in question. The metal is partly volatilized and partly melted, and gives rise to a disperse system. If the process takes place in gas, the particles settle on the walls of the vessel, forming coloured films. Such films were already obtained by van Marum (1787) (23), and very ingeniously studied by Faraday (1857) (24). If the process takes place near a liquid surface some of the particles can be collected in the liquid, forming a sol with it (25). If the metal is immersed in a liquid while the current is sent through it, a layer of vapour from the liquid around it will instantly be produced, so that the condensation of the metal vapour will take place partly in gas and partly on the liquid surface bounding the liquid vapour region. The condensate is collected in the liquid (25). Part of the melted metal is probably disintegrated and dispersed by the sudden movement of the liquid and the vapours from it. The volatilization may partly be caused by the Joule heat and partly by small electric arcs formed between parts of the wire at the moment of its melting. If the volatilization of the wire is carried out in a transverse magnetic field, the degree of dispersion of the colloid obtained seems to be a little higher than without such a field. Probably this is due to the very short duration of the arc in a transverse magnetic field.

Hence the metal vapour will be readily spread and condensed before it has time to form large particles.

Hitherto we have dealt with condensation processes occurring when vapours come into contact with gaseous, liquid or solid material at a lower temperature. In doing so, moreover, we have confined ourselves almost exclusively to the condensation of metal vapour. The experiences gained there may be applied to other cases, viz., the formation of colloid by condensation of non-metallic vapours. Such processes are, however, only very little studied as yet, and are, therefore, at present of little interest for our description of the formation of colloids. (Ehrenhaft prepared disperse systems in gases by condensation of sulphur vapour, and Westgren obtained a sulphur hydrosol by injecting sulphur vapour into water.)

Another very important case of formation of disperse systems by condensation in a gas is the condensation of supersaturated vapour by adiabatic expansion. In this case the whole volume of the vapour is *cooled all through and at once*, in contradistinction to the cases treated above, where the vapour was *cooled along the surfaces of contact* between the hot vapour and the cold material that it encountered. The latter class of processes may, therefore, suitably be called *surface condensation processes*, the former *volume condensation processes*.

In the cases of adiabatic condensation studied so far, one is dealing almost exclusively with condensation of vapours to liquid drops. The only case where the adiabatic expansion led to a disperse system with solid disperse phase is E. Meyer's experiment with regard to the condensation of water vapour in air under o° (26). Disperse systems formed by adiabatic expansions are rather unstable, as is generally the case with disperse systems in gases. These investigations have, however, given very important and detailed information as to the mechanism of the condensation process itself, and are, accordingly, of great interest for the chemistry of colloids.

We shall first consider the phenomena to be observed in connection with the condensation of water vapour in air (27). If a volume v_1, saturated with water vapour at, *e.g.*, $+ 20°$, is exposed to a series of adiabatic expansions, the cooling will increase as the ratio of volumes $\frac{v_2}{v_1}$ increases, v_2 being the volume of the vapour at the end of the expansion. Hence the supersaturation of the water vapour immediately after the expansion will increase with $\frac{v_2}{v_1}$. If condensation takes place it will go on until so much water is condensed that the heat set free by this process makes the remaining water vapour just saturated at the temperature attained. The diagram (Fig. 12) shows the maximal cooling t_2, the equilibrium temperature t_1, and the supersaturation S plotted against the ratio $\frac{v_2}{v_1}$ as abscissa. Here $S = \frac{\rho_1}{\rho_2}$ when ρ_1 denotes grammes of water per cubic centimetre immediately after expansion and ρ_2 the equilibrium concentration of water at the temperature t_2. The initial pressures are to be chosen so that after every expansion there shall be normal pressure (760 mm. mercury) in the gas. In Fig. 12 are also drawn the curve for the mass of water condensed per cubic centimetre (q_1) and the curve for the percentage of water condensed ($= \frac{q}{\rho_1} . 100$).

We will now consider more closely the condensation at various degrees of supersaturation. In a pure mixture of air and water vapour there is no condensation at supersaturations under about $4\cdot2\left(\dfrac{v_2}{v_1}<1\cdot25\right)$. If dust particles or products from chemical processes be present (*e.g.*, smoke particles or particles formed by the photochemical action of

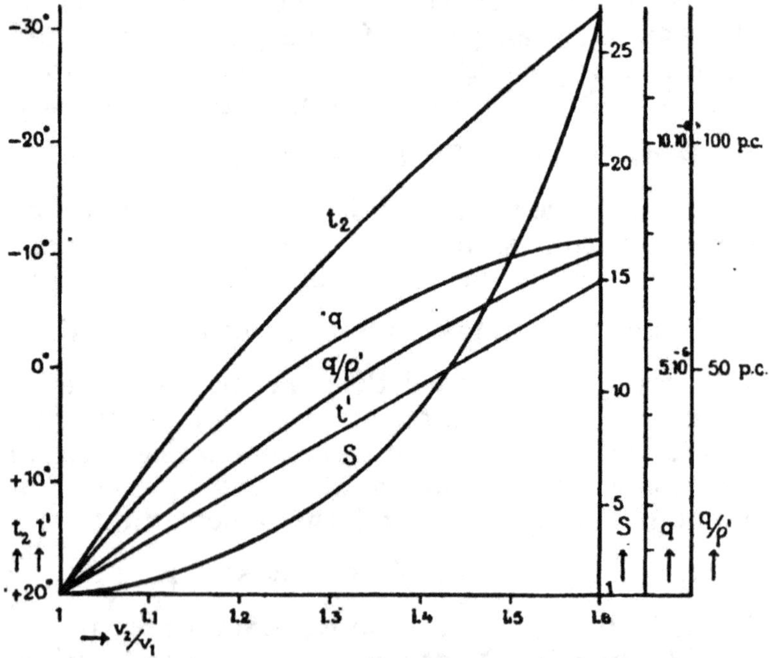

FIG. 12.—Variation of maximal cooling temperature t_2, equilibrium temperature t_1, supersaturation S, mass of water condensed per cubic centimetre q and percentage of water condensed q/ρ_1 with ratio of volumes v_2/v_1 in the case of condensation of water vapour by adiabatic expansion.

a strong illumination), water is condensed on these nuclei even at low supersaturation. Hence the degree of dispersion in this case depends entirely on the number of such nuclei present in the gas. In the pure air and water vapour mixture condensation begins at $S = 4\cdot2$, and, according to Wilson's investigations, it is the negative ions in the gas that serve as condensation centres. This form of condensation applies to the interval $S = 4\cdot2$ to 5 $\left(\dfrac{v_2}{v_1} = 1\cdot25 \text{ to } 1\cdot28\right)$.

Within the interval $S = 5\cdot8$ to $6\cdot8$ $\left(\dfrac{v_2}{v_1} = 1\cdot31 \text{ to } 1\cdot34\right)$ the positive ions act as condensation centres. As the " natural " ionization in air is very small, being caused in the main by the radioactivity of the earth and atmosphere, there are, under normal conditions, only a few centres in pure air that are able to act as condensation nuclei at supersaturations between $4\cdot2$ and $6\cdot8$. Hence the degree of dispersion of the system formed is very small. Accordingly, the condensate of that interval is called rain-like. The size of the drops varies from about $0\cdot2$ mm. in radius at $S = 4\cdot2$ to about $0\cdot02$ mm. at $S = 6\cdot8$, but the condensate always contains drops of rather different size. If the ionization is increased, for instance, by exposing the gas to X-rays or radium rays, the number of centres and, consequently, the degree of dispersion of the condensate are increased. In this way it is possible to produce within the interval $S = 4\cdot2$ to $6\cdot8$ dense fogs with small drops of rather uniform size. C. T. R. Wilson very ingeniously employed this process to make the paths of single a- and β-particles visible (28). Passing on to still higher degrees of supersaturation, we find a very rapid increase in the degree of dispersion of the condensate at $S = 8$. The condensate is now fog-like. When the supersaturation 12 is reached, the number of drops formed per cubic centimetre does not increase any longer, but remains constant. As the mass of water condensed still increases, the degree of dispersion begins to decrease slowly from the value $S = 12$. The radius of the drops at $S = 12$ is about $0\cdot6\,\mu$, and is fairly uniform through the whole system. The diagram (Fig. 13) shows the mass of condensate per cubic centimetre (q) as a function of the supersaturation (S). In the diagram are also plotted a series of measurements of the number of drops per cubic centimetre (N) at various degrees of supersaturation (29). This latter curve illustrates very well the change in the degree of dispersion of the condensate with increasing supersaturation. The values of N certainly refer to condensates of some-

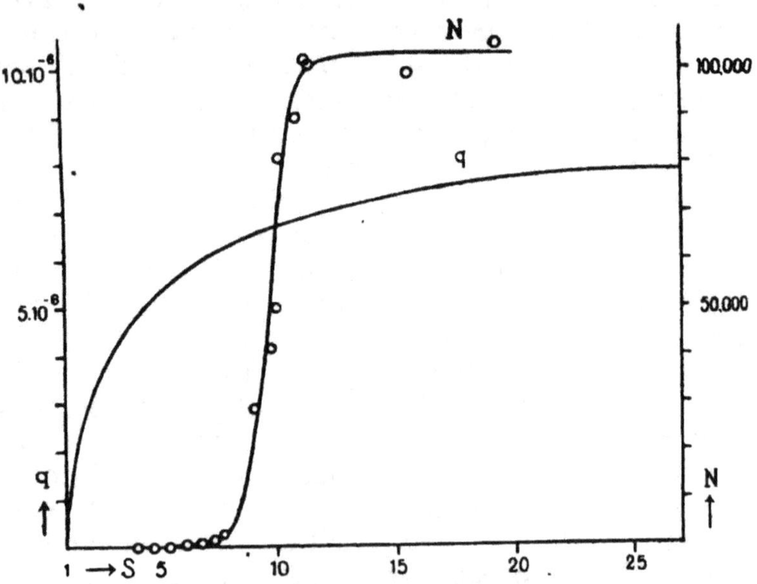

Fig. 13.—Variation of mass of condensate q and number of drops N per cubic centimetre with supersaturation S in the case of condensation of water vapour by adiabatic expansion.

what different total masses, but, as the q curve shows, this mass only varies very little within the interval of observation ($S = 4 \cdot 2$ to $19 \cdot 3$). As to the nature of these very numerous nuclei which begin to act at $S = 8$, and of which the number for water vapour in air is about 100,000 per cubic centimetre, it has been stated that they are electrically neutral and are very probably derived from the water vapour and not from the air. Experiments with other gases, viz., hydrogen and carbon dioxide, instead of air have given quite the same values for N within the interval $S = 8$ to 15. Within the region $S = 4 \cdot 2$ to $6 \cdot 8$, N is to some degree dependent on the nature of the gas. This phenomenon is explained by the fact that the natural ionization varies in different cases. According to P. Lenard the condensation centres in the interval $S = 8$ to 15 are complex water molecules (30).

The condensation by adiabatic expansion of vapours other than water has been studied especially by Andrén, and it has been stated that on the whole the process takes place in the same way (31). The constants of the process are, however, different and characteristic for each substance. Thus the values of S where highly disperse condensates just begin to be formed for methyl alcohol, ethyl alcohol, propyl alcohol and benzene are $4 \cdot 0$, $2 \cdot 5$, $3 \cdot 5$ and $11 \cdot 0$ respectively. The maximal number of drops per cubic centimetre is 160,000, 340,000, 360,000 and 190,000 respectively.

It is obvious that these results are of great importance for our views as to other kinds of condensation processes in gases. The existence of certain critical degrees of supersaturation characteristic of the various substances, above which the degree of dispersion of the formed system becomes high, is probably not confined to condensation caused by adiabatic expansion. It is very probably a phenomenon common to most forms of condensation in gases.

The supersaturation necessary for the formation of a disperse system in a gas may also be produced by the formation of a new substance by chemical reaction. The new substance must, of course, be present at the moment of formation in a molecular state, *i.e.*, as gas in a gas, and, provided the concentration be great enough, this represents a supersaturation.

Two cases must be taken into consideration. Either the condensation takes place simultaneously in the whole volume of the gas (volume condensation), or it takes place along certain surfaces within the gas (surface condensation). We have examples of the former case in the formation of disperse systems by photochemical reactions, of the latter in the production of smoke by the mixing together of certain gases, $e.g.$, $HCl + NH_3$. When gases which react on one another to form a solid or liquid phase are mixed, it may of course be possible for the condensation process to take place in a homogeneous system and, consequently, simultaneously throughout the whole gas volume. But such a case assumes that the mixing process is carried out very quickly and that the supersaturation lasts long enough for the system to become quite homogeneous—a condition very rarely realized in practice.

The formation of disperse systems in gases by such processes has so far been studied only very slightly. Tyndall made some interesting experiments on the formation of highly disperse fogs by photochemic reactions (32). A glass tube about $\frac{1}{2}$ metre in length and 6 to 8 cm. in diameter was filled with a photochemically sensitive gas mixture that could give rise to some non-volatile reaction product. Air with a slight trace of amyl nitrite gas and a little hydrochloric gas proved to be very suitable. An intense beam of light from an arc lamp was then thrown into the tube along its axis. In the glass tube, at first optically empty, there arose after a minute or so a blue fog, made visible by the illuminating beam of light, and this fog gradually became more dense and at the same time more and more white in colour. At last the tube contained a thick white fog. The light diffused by the fog was at first totally polarized in a plane perpendicular to the axis of the tube, but as the fog became more and more white the nonpolarized part became more prominent. Obviously we are dealing here with a disperse system that passes from a high degree of dispersion to a low one.

In general, the degree of dispersion seems to be higher in volume condensation than in surface condensation. Thus the Tyndall fogs are relatively highly disperse, while ammonium chloride smoke formed by mixing ammonia gas and hydrochloric gas is less disperse. The latter is thought to be a surface condensation, the former a volume condensation process.

The smoke formed by the incomplete combustion of bituminous coals, *i.e.*, hydrocarbons of high carbon percentage, may be regarded as the production of a disperse system in a gaseous medium by a condensation process preceded by a chemical dissociation. The particles act as nuclei for the condensation of water vapour even at low degrees of supersaturation (*cf.* p. 44), and thus give rise to those dirty fogs from which great towns in damp climates, *e.g.*, London, are suffering.

Real dispersion processes leading to the formation of disperse systems in gases are very incompletely known. The degree of dispersion is on the whole rather low. In this category we have the *mechanical pulverization of a liquid by means of a gas jet* (sprayer, Schoop's metallization process (33)), and by *means of a hard surface* against which the liquid is thrown (rain beating against a rock), *grinding of solid bodies* (starch dust in mills, ore dust in bucking-mills). Of much greater interest is the formation and disintegration of that peculiar form of disperse systems which is represented by bubbles and foam. If a gas is set free in a liquid to a concentration above saturation, or if it is injected into the liquid from outside, it will of course rise to the surface

It differs from it in the following respect: The production of colloid is much greater in the case of the wave current arc. For 1 ampere it is about three times as great. The decomposition for 1 ampere is, however, only increased to about double, so that the specific decomposition, *i.e.*, the ratio between decomposition and loss in weight of electrodes, is smaller in the case of the wave current arc. The order of the various metals, arranged according to the total loss in weight of electrodes per minute, is not quite the same in the case of the wave current as in that of the damped oscillatory current arc. In Table 4 some figures demonstrating this fact are given.

TABLE 4.

Current intensity $= 1 \cdot 5$ ampere.

Oscillatory current arc; capacity = 0·003 m.f.		Wave current arc; capacity = 0·013 m.f.	
Metal.	Total loss in weight of electrodes in milligrammes per minute.	Metal.	Total loss in weight of electrodes in milligrammes per minute.
Pb . .	45	Sb . .	130
Bi . .	33	Bi . .	75
Sb . .	25	Pb . .	64
Cd . .	21	Cd . .	48
Zn . .	8	Zn . .	25
Au . .	6	Au . .	10
Pt . .	3	Pt . .	4
Al . .	2	Ag . .	2·6
Ag . .	1·3	Cu . .	2·0
Cu . .	1·0	Al . .	0·1

The loss in weight of electrodes is not equally divided between cathode and anode, but the anode loses more than the cathode. With increasing length of arc this difference becomes less marked. The ratio between dispersion and condensation product is a little less than in the case of the damped oscillatory arc. The secondary degree of dispersion of the colloid formed is about the same as in the case of the damped oscillatory arc, but macroscopic coagulation often takes place during or immediately after the formation.

Another method of preparing disperse systems with metal as disperse phase, which is clearly related to the process just described, consists in passing an electric current of high intensity through a foil or wire of the metal in question. The metal is partly volatilized and partly melted, and gives rise to a disperse system. If the process takes place in gas, the particles settle on the walls of the vessel, forming coloured films. Such films were already obtained by van Marum (1787) (23), and very ingeniously studied by Faraday (1857) (24). If the process takes place near a liquid surface some of the particles can be collected in the liquid, forming a sol with it (25). If the metal is immersed in a liquid while the current is sent through it, a layer of vapour from the liquid around it will instantly be produced, so that the condensation of the metal vapour will take place partly in gas and partly on the liquid surface bounding the liquid vapour region. The condensate is collected in the liquid (25). Part of the melted metal is probably disintegrated and dispersed by the sudden movement of the liquid and the vapours from it. The volatilization may partly be caused by the Joule heat and partly by small electric arcs formed between parts of the wire at the moment of its melting. If the volatilization of the wire is carried out in a transverse magnetic field, the degree of dispersion of the colloid obtained seems to be a little higher than without such a field. Probably this is due to the very short duration of the arc in a transverse magnetic field.

Hence the metal vapour will be readily spread and condensed before it has time to form large particles.

Hitherto we have dealt with condensation processes occurring when vapours come into contact with gaseous, liquid or solid material at a lower temperature. In doing so, moreover, we have confined ourselves almost exclusively to the condensation of metal vapour. The experiences gained there may be applied to other cases, viz., the formation of colloid by condensation of non-metallic vapours. Such processes are, however, only very little studied as yet, and are, therefore, at present of little interest for our description of the formation of colloids. (Ehrenhaft prepared disperse systems in gases by condensation of sulphur vapour, and Westgren obtained a sulphur hydrosol by injecting sulphur vapour into water.)

Another very important case of formation of disperse systems by condensation in a gas is the condensation of supersaturated vapour by adiabatic expansion. In this case the whole volume of the vapour is *cooled all through and at once*, in contradistinction to the cases treated above, where the vapour was *cooled along the surfaces of contact* between the hot vapour and the cold material that it encountered. The latter class of processes may, therefore, suitably be called *surface condensation processes*, the former *volume condensation processes*.

In the cases of adiabatic condensation studied so far, one is dealing almost exclusively with condensation of vapours to liquid drops. The only case where the adiabatic expansion led to a disperse system with solid disperse phase is E. Meyer's experiment with regard to the condensation of water vapour in air under $0°$ (26). Disperse systems formed by adiabatic expansions are rather unstable, as is generally the case with disperse systems in gases. These investigations, have, however, given very important and detailed information as to the mechanism of the condensation process itself, and are, accordingly, of great interest for the chemistry of colloids.

We shall first consider the phenomena to be observed in connection with the condensation of water vapour in air (27). If a volume v_1, saturated with water vapour at, *e.g.*, $+ 20°$, is exposed to a series of adiabatic expansions, the cooling will increase as the ratio of volumes $\frac{v_2}{v_1}$ increases, v_2 being the volume of the vapour at the end of the expansion. Hence the supersaturation of the water vapour immediately after the expansion will increase with $\frac{v_2}{v_1}$. If condensation takes place it will go on until so much water is condensed that the heat set free by this process makes the remaining water vapour just saturated at the temperature attained. The diagram (Fig. 12) shows the maximal cooling t_2, the equilibrium temperature t_1, and the supersaturation S plotted against the ratio $\frac{v_2}{v_1}$ as abscissa. Here $S = \frac{\rho_1}{\rho_2}$ when ρ_1 denotes grammes of water per cubic centimetre immediately after expansion and ρ_2 the equilibrium concentration of water at the temperature t_2. The initial pressures are to be chosen so that after every expansion there shall be normal pressure (760 mm. mercury) in the gas. In Fig. 12 are also drawn the curve for the mass of water condensed per cubic centimetre (q_1) and the curve for the percentage of water condensed ($= \frac{q}{\rho_1} \cdot 100$).

We will now consider more closely the condensation at various degrees of supersaturation. In a pure mixture of air and water vapour there is

FORMATION OF DISPERSE SYSTEMS IN LIQUIDS AND IN SOLIDS.

CONDENSATION PROCESSES.

THE supersaturation necessary for condensation in a liquid medium may be caused by *cooling*, by adding a reagent that *lowers the solubility* of some substance dissolved in the medium, or by *producing the material of the disperse phase* (e.g., by a chemical reaction) in a concentration high in relation to its solubility.

The formation of disperse systems according to the first principle has not yet been subjected to exhaustive investigation. The cooling cannot be brought about, as in the case of the adiabatic expansion of a gas, simultaneously in the whole volume of the liquid, but must be conducted through the liquid. The condensation therefore becomes to some extent a surface condensation, but in practice it may very nearly approach volume condensation, provided the cooling be conducted rapidly enough through the liquid. Some examples may be mentioned. The cooling with ice of a solution of benzene in water saturated at boiling heat gives a benzene colloid, *i.e* a benzene-hydrosol. By placing an alcoholic solution of sulphur in contact with liquid air we get a sulphur-alcosol (1). A solution of water in pentane under the same conditions gives an ice-pentanosol (2), etc. When such a " cryosol " is slowly warmed up, the condensation process at first proceeds by lowering the degree of dispersion of the system, but as the solubility of the disperse phase rises, a point is reached where a kind of dispersion process sets in, the size of the particles, *i.e.*, the degree of dispersion of the system, being reduced by re-solution of the particles. P. P. von Weimarn has observed the following phenomenon. If a test tube containing some cubic centimetres of an alcoholic solution of sulphur is dipped in liquid air, the solution freezes to a clear glass, which no doubt contains the sulphur partly in a supersaturated molecular form and partly in a highly disperse colloid form. If the test tube is then taken out of the liquid air and slowly warmed, there appears at first a slight blue opalescence, which soon becomes stronger and more whitish. As the temperature rises still more the opalescence diminishes, turns blue and pale as at the beginning, and at last quite vanishes. The slight bluish opalescence at the beginning corresponds to the small particles formed by condensation, the white colour is due to the particles growing greater and greater, and ·the returning of the blue opalescence means the diminishing of their size by re-solution (dispersion), which ultimately leads to their returning entirely to the molecular state. A quantitative investigation of the various degrees of dispersion obtained by cooling such systems to various temperatures would be of great interest. If the experiment is arranged so as to cause the cooling to take place very rapidly and uniformly throughout the whole system, an analogy would thus be established with the investigations in gases of the variation of the degree of dispersion with the degree of supersaturation.

Condensation by means of a substance that lowers the solubility of the material of the future disperse phase is also a simple form of condensation that might be worth studying more closely. If a solution of palmitic acid is injected into water the solubility of the acid is reduced, and consequently a supersaturation is created that leads to precipitation of high disperse palmitic acid (3). The degree of dispersion depends on the magnitude of the supersaturation and on the speed with which it is effected, *i.e.*, on the rate of supersaturation. P. P. von Weimarn in an analogous way prepared disperse systems of sulphur, phosphorus and selenium (4).

It is probable that we must regard the electrolytic pulverizing of metals, studied especially by Haber (5), as a peculiar case of lowering of solubility. If an alkaline solution is electrolysed with a lead cathode, there occurs a sort of pulverizing of the cathode, brown clouds of metallic lead emanating from it. In an acid solution a similar but less marked phenomenon is to be observed. In the former case Haber has shown that an alloy is formed between the cathode metal and the alkali metal set free by the current, and this alloy is then decomposed by the water. The solvent of the lead solution, *i.e.*, the alkali metal, is thus removed and the lead is left behind in the water, in which it is almost insoluble, as a disperse system. Probably the phenomenon consists in a condensation of lead molecules to colloid particles and lead lamellæ, the latter disintegrating into particles as the condensation goes on. In the case of electrolysis in acid solution the hydrogen very likely plays the part of the alkali metal. We may perhaps equally well assume that at first a hydride is formed and that this compound is decomposed by the water. If such be the case this phenomenon should come under the heading "Dissociation (p. 90).

A process quite analogous to the cathode-pulverization in alkaline solutions takes place, as Haber has proved, when water is allowed to act upon certain alloys of alkali metals and various other metals. The phenomenon can easily be observed if fragments of a sodium-lead alloy are thrown into water.

The most important and as yet most exhaustively

studied processes giving rise to disperse systems are those in which the material of the disperse phase is produced in high concentration. Most commonly this is effected by means of a *chemical reaction*, but other forms, too, are known. Thus colloids of radio-active substances are often formed by the element itself being produced within the system.

Here also it may be useful to bear in mind the two cases of condensation, viz., volume condensation and surface condensation. An example of the former case in its pure form is the formation of colloid sulphur in an alcoholic solution by means of ultra-violet illumination (transformation into another allotropic modification). All condensation by photo-reaction is more or less a volume condensation. When solutions that react with each other are mixed, in most cases surface condensation at the contact surface between the solutions takes place. If the condensation or the reaction proceed slowly enough, volume condensation may occur even in this case. Pure volume condensation most probably gives rise to systems of a more homogeneous degree of dispersion than mixed surface and volume condensation. The pure surface condensation very likely produces systems with rather unequal particles. The degree of super-saturation at different points in the limit layer between the solutions will depend on the diffusion, *i.e.*, on the time and on the distance from the first contact surface.

As regards the classification of the various forms of condensation processes arising from chemical reactions, we may, according to the kind of reaction, put them under one of the following headings :—

Reduction.
Oxidation.
Dissociation.
Double decomposition.

Perhaps it would be more rational to choose for

the purpose of classification characteristic features from the condensation process itself and not from the chemical reaction that precedes the condensation. Such a form of classification we have in the two groups : condensation with spontaneous formation of nuclei ; condensation with addition of nuclei. The degree of supersaturation might also be taken as a basis of classification.

Now in most cases we know only very little of the mechanism of the condensation process. Thus it appears that for the present it will be best to adhere to the classification according to the chemical reaction, especially as a close study of the proper reactions and the condensation processes accompanying them may very likely be the only way to arrive at the general laws of condensation.

As stated above, we must distinguish between the primary, the secondary and the tertiary degree of dispersion. The primary degree of dispersion being commonly the highest, it is obvious that the methods of preparation in most cases aim at suppressing those processes which lead to secondary or tertiary degree of dispersion. The chief methods of attaining this are :—

1. Very low solubility of the disperse phase in the dispersion medium.
2. Suitable (not too high) ion concentrations.
3. Low concentration of the disperse phase.
4. Low temperature.
5. The presence of a protective colloid.

Conditions such as those just mentioned may, however, in some cases influence the condensation process in such a way as to form a less high *primary* degree of dispersion. We then get the optimum conditions in the form of a compromise.

In cases where these conditions are not fulfilled and coagulation therefore takes place, the primary structure may often be regained by—

1. Lowering the concentration of the ions present (washing).
2. Replacing unsuitable ions by suitable ones (washing and peptization).

The two latter processes were previously considered as dispersion processes, but recent investigations have shown that they are in general only reversible coagulations. The degree of dispersion is not altered, only the distribution of the particles in the dispersion medium is changed.

The removal of electrolytes from colloid solutions may be carried out in different ways. There is the simple washing of the coagulum on a filter or by sedimentation and decanting, the filtration through collodion or gelatin membranes, which permit the crystalloids to pass freely but retain the colloids (ultra-filtration) (6), Graham's classical dialysis (7), and lastly electrolysis (8). The methods of ultra-filtration and dialysis have of late been considerably improved and now constitute a very important procedure in the preparation of colloids (9).

There is a large and very important class of disperse systems, most probably formed by condensation processes, concerning the mechanism of formation of which we are still almost ignorant, viz., the organic colloids, especially those found in plants and animals. Owing to the investigations of E. Fischer (10), we know, for instance, that the proteins are built up of amino-acids, but the conditions under which they give rise to those highly disperse colloids that play such a prominent part in the organic world have not yet been elucidated. Some of them may be completely dried and yet redissolve to hydrosols when brought in contact with water. Many salts of organic substances form colloid solutions in water but crystalline solutions in organic solvents, *e.g.*, alcohol, benzene. In some cases the process may be regarded as a hydrolysis. The formation of hydrosols of many dyestuffs comes under this heading (10a). On the other hand, there are dyestuffs that form hydrosols when dissolved in water which are certainly not hydrolysed to any noticeable degree. The alkali salts of the higher fatty acids seem to be almost completely hydrolysed in concentrated aqueous solutions, while they are not so much hydrolysed in dilute solutions, quite contrary to the experience with inorganic salts. It cannot be a hydrolysis equilibrium of the ordinary kind, as such solutions show no raising of the boiling point, notwithstanding their content of " free " alkali (11).

The swelling and redissolution of, *e.g.*, gelatin, and the colloid dissolution of dyestuffs might be considered as a kind of dispersion process. The structure or degree of dispersion brought about were, however, probably latent in the substance before it came in contact with the solvent, and the process is therefore probably to be looked upon as a change of state in the system and not as a formation of a new disperse system.

Reduction.

The best known reduction process is the reduction of chlorauric acid ($HAuCl_4$) to gold. Almost every conceivable reducing agent has been studied, viz., hydrogen, hydrogen peroxide, hydrogen sulphide, carbon monoxide, carbon disulphide, nitric oxide, phosphorus, phosphorus tetroxide, hypophosphoric acid, sulphur dioxide, sodium thiosulphate, sodium bisulphite, ferrous sulphate, tin, stannous chloride, acetylene, terpenes, alcohols, glycerine, aldehydes, acrolein, oxalic acid and oxalates, tartaric acid, sugars, starches, phenols, hydroxide acids, hydro-chinones, hydrazines, hydroxylamines, protalbic acid, electric sparks (formation of nitric oxide), α-, β- and γ-rays, etc., etc. (12). In spite of these extensive investigations we know but very little of the mechanism of the reducing process itself. It still remains to be settled in which stages it takes place, what are the intermediate products, whether it is independent of the condensation that follows, etc.

As to the reducing process itself it seems to proceed differently in a *pure* (or acid) and in an *alkaline* solution. The simplest and most easily studied case is reduction with hydrogen peroxide in a pure solution of $HAuCl_4$:

$$2HAuCl_4 + 3H_2O_2 = 2Au + 8HCl + 3O_2 \quad (13).$$

Here neither the reducing agent itself nor the products formed, except the hydrochloric acid, are electrolytes. Hence we may easily follow the course of the reduction by measuring the electric conductivity of the solution. This quantity will rise during the reduction process from the value for $HAuCl_4$ at the dilution in question to the value for $4HCl$ at the same dilution. Measurements carried out by H. Nordenson (14) and by the writer have brought out the following facts.

First case : No nuclei are present at the beginning of the reduction. When the reducing agent is added there is a sudden increase in conductivity of about 30 per cent. (A—B, Fig. 14). At the same time the yellow colour of the solution decreases considerably. Then the conductivity rises for some time very slowly or remains almost constant, and so does the colour too (B—C in Fig. 14). After this period there follows one of rapid rise in the conductivity (C—D in Fig. 14), accompanied by a sudden red coloration of the liquid. When examined in the ultra-microscope the system at this period is seen to contain a great number of particles, none of which were present during the stages A—B and B—C. When the intensity of colour no longer increases the conductivity has likewise attained its limiting value for $4HCl$.

Second case : Nuclei are present at the beginning of the reduction. From the addition of the reducing agent to the end of the reduction the conductivity as well as the colour intensity now increases almost proportional to time (Fig. 14, A—D'). If nuclei are added to the reduction mixture during the stage B—C we get an intermediate case represented by the curve A—B—C″—D″.

As to the explanation of these phenomena the following hypothesis suggests itself. The part A—B of the curve denotes reduction of about $\frac{1}{3}$ of the

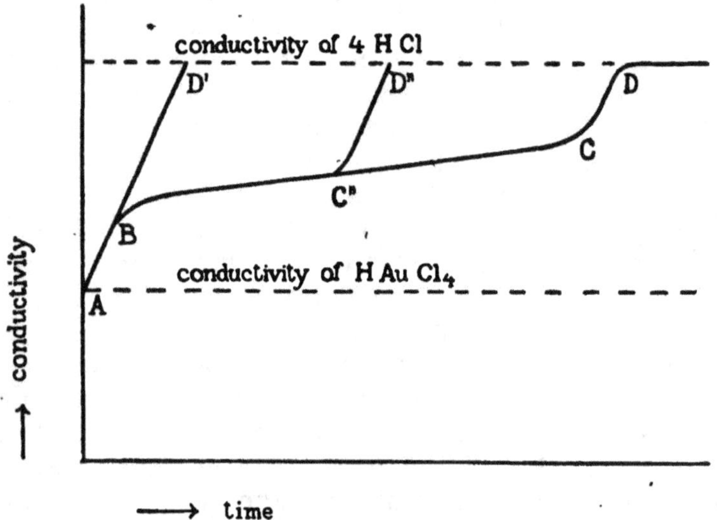

FIG. 14.—Variation of conductivity with time when reducing chlorauric acid with hydrogen peroxide.

$HAuCl_4$ to Au. Hereby a highly supersaturated solution of gold is formed and the progress of the reduction is stopped according to the law of mass-action. The solubility of gold in water being of course very low, viz., less than 10^{-9}, the degree of supersaturation will prove to be quite enormous, viz., 10^7 at a concentration of 10^{-3} normal. Most probably this enormous supersaturation gives rise to a disperse system of an exceedingly high degree of dispersion. As the condensation proceeds, the small primary particles being aggregated or coagulated to secondary particles, the reduction goes on slowly along the part B—C of the curve. When the size of the greater number of particles has reached a certain value they begin to act as centres of condensation for molecular gold (at C in Fig. 14), and then the process is finished along the straight line C—D. The addition of nuclei at B or at C″ will only have the effect of displacing the part C—D to B—D′ or to C″—D″. In support of this hypothesis we may mention the observation made by Zsigmondy and by others that gold particles do not act as condensation nuclei unless their diameter has reached a certain value, viz., about 2 $\mu\mu$ (15).

The reduction of $HAuCl_4$ by hydrogen peroxide with the addition of nuclei has in recent years become of great value to the physics and chemistry of colloids (16). Two important applications are to be noted. Firstly, it is possible to prepare series of gold colloids with various degrees of dispersion by adding various amounts of gold nuclei to the reduction mixture. Secondly, the degree of dispersion of gold colloids with very small (amicroscopic) particles may be determined by immersing the particles in the reduction mixture and allowing them to grow large enough for ultra-microscopic investigation. Recently Börjeson (17) has shown that a great many other kinds of small particles act as nuclei in the reduction of gold by hydrogen peroxide, viz., metals such as platinum, silver, mercury, tin, copper, bismuth, cadmium, zinc, iron, aluminium, sulphides of antimony and arsenic, sulphur. Oxides of tin, iron and silicon as well as dyes and organic colloids, *e.g.*, gelatin and gum arabic, do not act as nuclei. When dealing with these " nuclei methods," whether it is a question of preparing a gold colloid of a certain degree of dispersion or of determining the degree of dispersion of a colloid—the particles of which are too small to be measured with the ultra-microscope—the fundamental condition is that there should be no spontaneous production of nuclei in the reduction mixture. According to Westgren the concentration of the $HAuCl_4$ should not be less than 10^{-4} normal and the number of nuclei added not less than $5 \cdot 10^{-9}$ per cubic centimetre, otherwise spontaneous production of gold nuclei will take place before the reduction is completed.

That under suitable conditions no spontaneous nuclei appear is demonstrated by the following table (5) given by Westgren :—

TABLE 5.

Cubic centimetres gold nuclei fluid ($= K'$.	Number of Particles formed per 10^{-8} cc. ($= n$).	$n/K.$
·8	121	15·1
12	169	14·1
16	231	14·4
20	289	14·5

Even in the case of nuclei of material other than gold the process may be carried out in such a manner that all the gold from the solution is deposited on the nuclei. A table given by Börjeson shows this.

TABLE 6.

Nuclei : Cadmium, prepared by the damped high-frequency alternating current arc in ethyl alcohol at $- 70°$ C.

Volume Cd—sol in the reduction experiment per 50 c.c. reduction mixture.	Radius of the nuclei as determined by the reduction experiment and the measurement of the degree of dispersion of the gold sol formed.
0·2 C.C.	11·4 $\mu\mu$
0·1 C.C.	10·7 $\mu\mu$
0·05 C.C.	11·0 $\mu\mu$
0·025 C.C.	10·9 $\mu\mu$

The method has not yet been sufficiently worked out and we may still expect to make much progress by means of a careful examination.

In order to get rid of the main part of the HCl formed by the reduction dialysis or filtration through collodion membranes may be used. In consequence of the great sensitiveness of gold hydrosols to small electrolytic impurities partial coagulation will often occur when they are dialysed. Gold hydrosols of not too high a degree of dispersion may be purified by repeated sedimentation and by replacing the dispersion medium by pure water. In this manner Westgren was able to prepare gold hydrosols almost free from HCl.

In those cases where alkali is added to the gold solution before reduction gold hydroxide is probably formed first and then an alkali auric salt (18). The reduction process will thus consist in precipitating the gold from the solution of this salt. The reaction between the chlorauric acid and the alkali may be written in the following manner.

$$HAuCl_4 + 4KOH = Au(OH)_3 + 4HCl + H_2O$$
$$Au(OH)_3 + KOH = KAuO_2 + 2H_2O$$

or

$$HAuCl_4 + 2K_2CO_3 + 2H_2O = Au(OH)_3 + 2CO_2 + 4KCl$$
$$2Au(OH)_3 + K_2CO_3 = 2KAuO_2 + 3H_2O + CO_2.$$

If formaldehyde be added we have

$$2KAuO_2 + 3HCHO + KOH = 2Au + 3HCOOK + 2H_2O$$

or

$$2KAuO_2 + 3HCHO + K_2CO_3 = 2Au + 3HCOOK + KHCO_3 + H_2O.$$

This agrees with the statement of Vanino that 2 mol. Au requires 11 mol. NaOH for reduction (19). Naumoff has prepared $KAuO_2$ and has shown that the solutions of this salt are reduced in the same way as mixtures of $HAuCl_4$ and alkali.

Even when we have to deal with " pure " solutions of $HAuCl_4$ there will always be present small quantities of $Au(OH)_3$, formed from the $HAuCl_4$ by hydrolysis. This decomposition of the gold solution is accelerated by light (20). At high degrees of dilution it may in time lead to a complete liberation of all the hydrochloric acid. The $Au(OH)_3$ being only sparingly soluble in water, a colloid solution of this gold compound is formed. The properties of the gold colloid prepared by reduction of this $Au(OH)_3$-sol will of course depend on the state of the latter.

The degree of dispersion of gold colloids formed by reduction of $HAuCl_4$ without the addition of condensation nuclei is, according to Zsigmondy (21), dependent on two factors, viz. :

1. The spontaneous production of nuclei (s.p.n.).

2. The velocity of growth of the particles (v.g.p.).

This means applying to the formation of colloids the view held by Tammann concerning crystallization in fused substances, and it seems, at least in the present state of research, to be of considerable value for the classification of the phenomena observed in the process of the formation of gold colloids by reduction.

The greater the number of gold nuclei produced the higher the degree of dispersion, and the sooner the nuclei are produced in the course of the reduction process the more uniform will be the size of the particles. Great velocity of growth will generally depress the degree of dispersion of the system, as there is not sufficient time for the production of nuclei before the gold supply of the solution is already exhausted. Of course this view holds good only for the primary degree of dispersion. The secondary degree of dispersion will, moreover, depend on the presence of coagulating and protective substances in the solution.

Zsigmondy's school has devoted much time and energy to finding out the influence of various substances added to the gold reduction mixture. It is impossible, however, to formulate any general laws, and the conclusions drawn by the various investigators do not hold when the experimental conditions are only slightly altered.

Hiege studied the reduction by formaldehyde in alkaline solution and obtained the following results (22). In pure water, freed with great care from contaminations, the reduction took place so rapidly that the formaldehyde could not even be completely mixed with the gold solution before the liquid was already coloured. The first particles formed before the mixing is completed will act as condensation nuclei and so will those formed a little later, etc. Hence the degree of dispersion becomes very heterogeneous. The process is a "surface condensation." With regard to the influence of substances added to the gold solution before reduction the following classes may be distinguished.

1. V.g.p. reduced.

Under this heading fall various colloids and high molecular substances, *e.g.*, gelatin, salts of protalbic acid, soaps, oils and fats ; among inorganic substances KBr, KJ have the same action but less pronounced.

The reduction is retarded whether gold particles (nuclei) be added or not. The degree of dispersion is in general increased by the substance added.

2. S.p.n. reduced.

Potassium ferro- and ferricyanide, ammonia and its salts have this effect.

Reduction is retarded if nuclei are not added, but is not retarded if nuclei are added.

3. S.p.n. accelerated.

Potassium thiocyanate, potassium oxalate, sodium citrate, congo red, benzopurpurine, and most inorganic salts in very low concentrations.

The reduction of $HAuCl_4$ in alkaline solution by hydrazine chlorhydrate (23) was studied by the

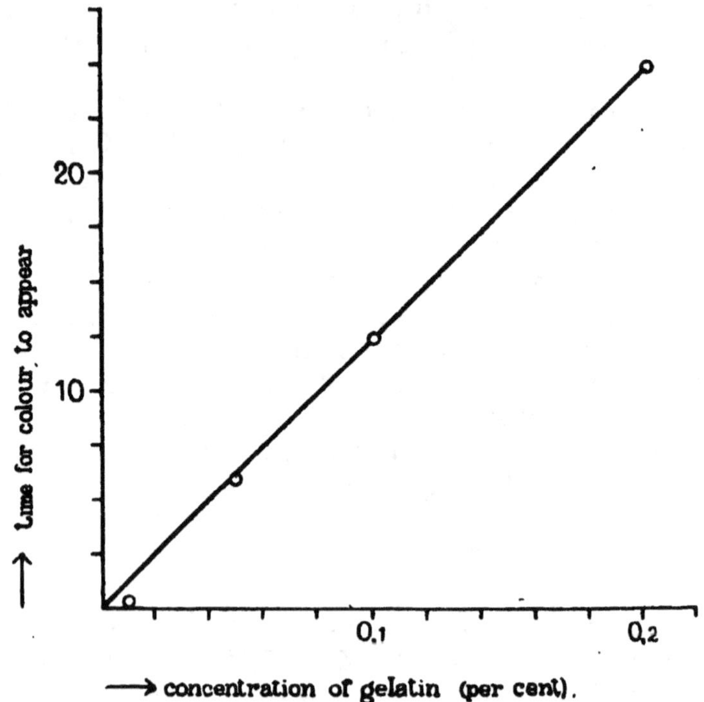

FIG. 15.—Variation of time required for the red colour to appear when reducing chlorauric acid in the presence of gelatin of various concentration.

writer at an early date (24). He found the appearance of the red colour retarded by gelatin, the retardation being almost proportional to the gelatin concentration (Fig. 15). When gelatin was present electrolytes were found to accelerate the appearance of the red colour, $MgCl_2$ being more effective than KCl and $BaCl_2$ more effective than $MgCl_2$. Nonelectrolytes, *e.g.*, urea, alcohol, glycerine, milk-sugar, pyridine, had no effect.

The observations of Hiege and of the writer may be interpreted as follows. The spontaneous production of gold nuclei is a kind of coagulation and is therefore accelerated by coagulating electrolytes in small quantities. Higher concentrations drive the aggregation of the particles too far. Weak reducing agents, *e.g.*, potassium thiocyanate, potassium citrate, congo red, etc., added before the reduction give rise to small gold particles which act as nuclei. Protective electrolytes, *e.g.*, NH_3, $K_4Fe(CN)_6$, $K_3Fe(CN)_6$, retard the production of nuclei. Protective colloids do not retard the s.p.n., their particles being too coarse for these very small gold particles. The growth of the particles is also a kind of coagulation. It is retarded by protective colloids and accelerated by coagulating electrolytes.

As to the nature of the protective action, it most probably consists in an absorption of the gold particles by the particles of the protective colloid,

TABLE 7.

Exposure (seconds).	Time for colour to appear (minutes).	Diameter ($\mu\mu$).
0	10	90
1	5	70
2	5	50
3	4	40
5	$\frac{1}{2}$	30
10	$\frac{1}{3}$	20
20	Very short.	10—15
30	Very short.	10
60	Very short.	10

e.g., gelatin, albumin, gum arabic, etc. This process takes a considerable time (order of magnitude :

some minutes) and thus it happens that the condensation is rather far advanced before the protective colloid has had time to come into full action.

H. Nordenson has shown that the reduction of $HAuCl_4$ to gold colloids by means of H_2O_2 is influenced by light (25). If a dilute solution of

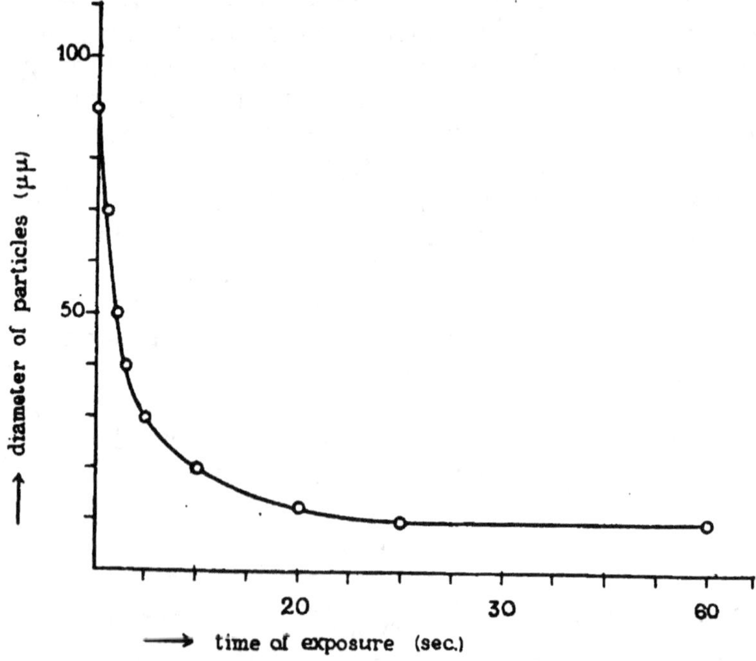

FIG. 16.—Variation of degree of dispersion with time of exposure in the case of reducing chlorauric acid with hydrogen peroxide and illuminating the reduction mixture with ultra-violet light.

$HAuCl_4$ is mixed with some drops of H_2O_2 and immediately exposed to the ultra-violet rays of a strong mercury vapour lamp the reduction is greatly accelerated and the degree of dispersion of the system formed is considerably higher than without light. The size of the particles at first increases very rapidly with the duration of exposure and then becomes constant (Table 7 and Fig. 16). A glass plate inserted between the lamp and the solution reduces the action of the light quite markedly, the diameter of the particles being in this case about 45 $\mu\mu$, instead of about 10 $\mu\mu$ without the glass plate. Thus the light action is mainly due to the ultra-violet rays.

A satisfactory explanation of this very remarkable phenomenon has not yet been found. According to Nordenson's experiments pure solutions of $HAuCl_4$ are only very slowly reduced by light and the disperse system formed has a low degree of dispersion, *i.e.*, the particles are rather large. Hence the phenomenon must be connected with condensation only and is very probably due to rapid formation of condensation nuclei by the light.

A reduction method that gives gold colloids of a very high degree of dispersion is Faraday's (26) classical process, improved by Zsigmondy (27). Here $HAuCl_4$ in slightly alkaline solution is reduced by phosphorus. In practice $HAuCl_4$ of about $1 \cdot 10^{-4}$ normal with about $5 \cdot 10^{-4}$ K_2CO_3 is mixed with some drops of an etheric solution of phosphorus. The reduction takes place very slowly, a day often being necessary for it to be completed. The diameter of the particles is about 5 $\mu\mu$ and can be reduced still more by the addition of gelatin to the reduction mixture. The mechanism of the process is rather complicated. Some low oxide of phosphorus is formed first, and this oxide acts as a reducing agent. The cause of the very high degree of dispersion is not yet known. Perhaps it may be attributed to the very rapid and abundant formation of ion nuclei accompanying the oxidation of phosphorus.

As a rule the greater the dilution of the $HAuCl_4$ the higher the degree of dispersion of the gold colloid (Fig. 17) (28). This law holds good for all sorts of gold reduction processes. The fact seems to be opposed to the general rule stated above, viz., the greater the supersaturation the higher the degree of dispersion. The explanation might be that in high dilutions the growth of the particles is much depressed. Hence more nuclei can be formed before the supply of gold is exhausted. Odén has suggested to the writer

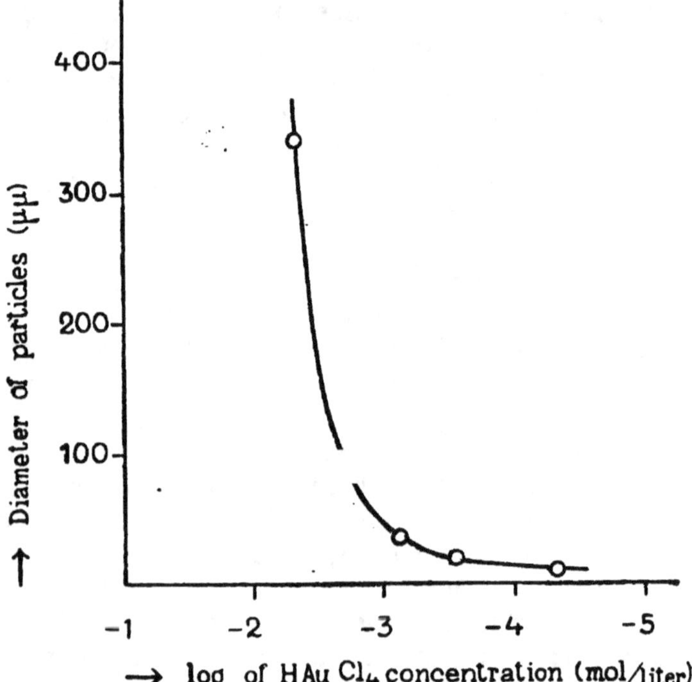

FIG. 17.—Variation of degree of dispersion with concentration in the case of formation of gold hydrosol by reduction of chlorauric acid.

that the velocity of reduction may be considerably diminished by the dilution, while the formation of nuclei, being very likely a coagulation process, may be diminished to a lesser extent.

The reduction of a gold salt to metallic gold may of course take place in some solvent other than water. A case that is of great interest both theoretically and practically is the formation of small gold particles in glass (29). It is not stated whether this reaction is a true reduction of gold salt by some component of the glass or a mere decomposition of it by heat. In any case we will deal with the case here as it shows a close analogy to the formation of gold hydrosols by reduction.

If a small quantity of a gold compound, *e.g.*, gold chloride, is added to a suitable glass at red heat (lead or barium glass) and the glass is allowed to cool slowly, a colourless glass is obtained, which becomes ruby red when heated again quickly (but not to melting). This red glass—gold ruby glass—as Zsigmondy and Siedentopf first showed, contains a great many ultra-microscopic gold particles (30). If a strip of the colourless gold glass is heated at one end there will be a certain fall of temperature along the glass strip in consequence of the thermal conduction. The result will be a glass with gold particles, the size of which decreases as the distance from the heat source increases. On the other hand, the number of particles per unit volume is constant through the whole strip. If the heating is continued further the glass again becomes colourless. Zsigmondy suggested the following explanation of these phenomena. At first the gold chloride is reduced to molecular metallic gold, which is kept in solution in the fused glass. By cooling the glass a considerable supersaturation is created and a condensation to very fine particles takes place, some of which reach the nucleus limit, *i.e.*, become large enough to act as nuclei. But, owing to the enormous viscosity of the glass at lower temperatures, these condensation centres do not grow. If the glass is quickly heated again, the system will enter into a region where the velocity of growth is great (the viscosity small). Hence the small invisible gold nuclei will grow to particles of ultra-microscopic size.

The experiment with the glass strip heated at one

end shows that the velocity of growth of the particles increases as the temperature rises and that the number of nuclei is not altered during the short period of reheating. At a somewhat higher temperature, however, the gold particles should be redissolved in the glass. Zsigmondy has tried to connect all these phenomena in the formation of gold ruby glass—as well as those in the formation of colloids by condensation in general—with some experiences of Tammann concerning crystallization in fused substances (31). Tammann found the production of crystallization centres to increase as the degree of supersaturation rises, then to reach a maximum, and finally to decrease with increasing supersaturation. The maximum velocity of growth does not in general coincide with the maximum production of nuclei. Generally it will be necessary to heat the melted matter to a temperature above the one at which the production of nuclei has its maximum in order to get a sufficient velocity of growth. It may, however, be doubted whether the crystallization and condensation in pure melted salt and in solutions really take place in so completely analogous a way that conclusions drawn from the one phenomenon may be applied to the other. At least, this must be done with great care and caution. Thus it ought to be mentioned that the number of nuclei produced in fused salt is only some hundred per cubic millimetre, while in gold ruby glass and in colloid solutions the number amounts to thousands of millions per cubic millimetre.

It is of some interest to notice that colloid gold formed by reduction had been known long before the idea of a colloid was originated (32). The "aurum potabile" of the alchemists was very probably a disperse system with gold as a disperse phase. Macquer, in his *Dictionnaire de Chymie*, second edition, Paris, 1774, tome 3, expresses a rather modern view on this subject, viz. : " However, all these gold tinctures are nothing but gold which is made extremely finely divided and floating in an oily fluid. They are therefore, properly speaking, no tinctures and, as stated by M. Le Baron in his Edition of Lemery's Chemistry, they may be called drinkable gold only so far as we connect with this name no other idea than the one that the gold is swimming in a fluid and is made into particles so fine that it may itself be regarded as potable in the form of a fluid."

Johann Juncher's *Conspectus Chemiæ* (" ins Teutsche übersetzt," Halle (1749)) contains many statements which point to the formation of gold colloids by reduction processes. In Table **XXXIII.** we read : " Even in the case when not more than a single drop of gold solution is distributed in some ounces of ordinary water so as to make it imperceptible both to sight and to smell the water will be coloured red everywhere as soon as a drop of tin-solution is added, which is to be regarded as a very clear statement of the extreme smallness of the particles."

In an essay published in London, 1794, Mrs. Fulhame made a very clear statement regarding the coloration of pieces of silk dipped in gold solution and treated with phosphorus or hydrogen (33). In the first part of the nineteenth century several investigators obtained red or purple liquids by the reduction of gold salts. Oberkampf (34) (1811), *e.g.*, treated dilute gold chloride with hydrogen and obtained liquids " *d'une belle couleur rouge pourpre, semblable à celle du vin . . . sans qu'il se formât aucun précipité.*"

Some very interesting remarks concerning the state of the gold in gold glass were made by J. B. Richter as early as 1802, and have recently been brought to light by Wilh. Ostwald. In the middle of the nineteenth century Faraday undertook his famous studies " On the experimental relations of gold to light," published in the *Trans. of the Roy. Soc.* (35).

Here the preparation of stable highly disperse gold hydrosols was described and the heterogeneous character of the red fluids clearly demonstrated. According to Faraday, " A quick and ready mode of producing the ruby fluid is to put a quart of the weak solution of gold (containing about 0·6 of a grain of metal) into a clean bottle, to add a little solution of phosphorus in ether, and then to shake it well for a few moments : a beautiful ruby or amethystine fluid is immediately produced, which will increase in depth of tint by a little time. Generally, however, the preparations made with phosphorus dissolved in sulphide of carbon are more ruby than those where ether is the phosphorous solvent. The process of reduction appears to consist in a transfer of the chlorine from the gold to the phosphorus and the formation of phosphorous acids and hydrochloric acid, by the further action of the water." The variation of the degree of dispersion with the dilution of the gold salt at the reduction, the formation of secondary particles (aggregates), and the necessity of using very clean vessels for the preparation of stable gold sols were also recognized by him. " Fluids thus prepared may differ much in appearance. Those from the basins, or from the stronger solution of gold, are often evidently turbid, looking brown or violet in different lights. Those prepared with weaker solutions and in bottles, are frequently more amethystine or ruby in colour and apparently clear. The latter, when in their finest state, often remain unchanged for many months and have all the appearance of solutions. But they never are such, containing in fact no dissolved but only diffused gold. The particles are easily rendered evident, by gathering the rays of the sun (or a lamp) into a cone by a lens, and sending the part of the cone near the focus into the fluid. The cone becomes visible, and though the illuminated particles cannot be distinguished because of their minuteness, yet the light they reflect is golden in character, and seen to be abundant in proportion to the quantity of solid gold present."

" A gradual change goes on amongst the particles diffused through these fluids, especially in the case where the gold is comparatively abundant. It appears to consist of an aggregation. Fluids, at first clear or almost clear to ordinary observation, become turbid ; being left to stand for a few days, a deposit falls."

" All the vessels used in these operations must be very clean ; though of glass they should not be supposed in proper condition after wiping, but should be soaked in water, and after that rinsed with distilled water. A glass supposed to be clean, and even a new bottle, is quite able to change the character of a given gold fluid."

Next to gold reduction, the reduction of silver attracts the attention. Silver compounds, especially AgOH and some organic silver compounds, are easily reduced.

The reduction of AgOH in aqueous solution by hydrogen is of especial interest for the theory of formation of colloids.

$$2AgOH + H_2 \rightarrow 2Ag + 2H_2O$$

This process was studied by Kohlschütter (36). He found that silver is deposited only at the surface of contact between the solution and the wall of the vessel containing it. The nature of this wall also has a considerable influence upon the degree of dispersion and other qualities of the colloid formed. Thus more fine-grained sols were obtained when the reduction was carried out in a vessel of quartz or ordinary glass than in one of Jena glass. When reduced in a platinum vessel the silver is deposited in form of crystals on the wall. Thus the degree of dispersion is the lowest for a platinum surface. Kohlschütter made use of this fact in order to purify his silver sols from AgOH. If a silver sol containing AgOH is poured into a platinized platinum basin and a current of hydrogen passed through the liquid for some hours, almost all the Ag of the AgOH is deposited on the wall of the vessel as silver crystals while the silver colloid is left unchanged.

The formation of silver mirrors by reduction of silver salts in solution is of interest in this connection. This process has also been studied by Kohlschütter (37). He found that the conditions for the deposition of the silver in the form of a mirror were slow velocity of reaction and the presence of certain high molecular and colloid substances, probably acting as protective colloids. The former condition may be fulfilled by using complex silver compounds. The mirror silver is probably built up of very fine particles deposited close to each other.

If the dilution of the silver salt be very great the formation of condensation nuclei is so diminished that no silver deposit takes place. This is the case when ammoniacal silver compounds are reduced by aldehyde in great dilution. Here Zsigmondy and Lottermoser found that gold particles added to the reduction mixture act as condensation centres (38). A silver colloid is formed with particles containing a small gold nucleus. Silver particles also act as condensation centres in most mixtures of silver compounds and reducing agents. The formation of the photographic image is probably due to such a process. Lüppo-Cramer obtained series of beautifully coloured silver sols by reducing silver nitrate (0·4 per cent.) at 25° C. with hydroquinone in the presence of gelatin (1 per cent.) and various quantities of silver nuclei (39). As the number of silver nuclei added increased, the particles in the system formed increased in number, and at the same time the colour changed : blue gray $\rightarrow$ blue $\rightarrow$ blue violet $\rightarrow$ ruby red $\rightarrow$ brownish yellow.

The great influence of small quantities of colloids on the formation of silver mirrors is also observed in case of hydrosol formation as a very high protective action. Such substances also raise the degree of dispersion of the system, as was the case with the gold hydrosols. Carey Lea's famous method of preparing colloid silver depends on this (40). Silver nitrate is reduced by ferrous citrate, and the deposit formed is dissolved in water and reprecipitated with ammonium nitrate.

$$\text{Ag} \cdot + \text{Fe} \cdot\cdot \rightarrow Ag + Fe \cdot\cdot\cdot$$

By precipitating the sols thus obtained with alcohol it is possible to get a substance containing 99 per cent. of silver, which forms a silver sol when brought in contact with water. The remainder is some ferrous colloid that acts as a protective colloid.

The silver hydrosols prepared according to Carey Lea's method contain particles of various sizes. Odén has shown that such a sol may be divided into a series of sols with particles of nearly equal size by means of fractional coagulation (41). As a coagulator Odén used ammonium nitrate in a concentration varying from 0·08 normal to 0·25 normal. The smallest particles require the highest concentration for coagulation.

Another form of reduction that has been studied by Kohlschütter in the case of silver is the electrolytic metal deposition (42). At the cathode there is at first formed a supersaturated solution of metallic silver, and the higher the silver concentration of the electrolyte and the current density, the higher the supersaturation will be. Thus we get black spongy deposits at high concentration and current density, and crystalline, glittering, compact deposits at low concentration and current density. The degree of dispersion observed is in most cases, however, a secondary one, and consequently it is very much influenced by coagulating factors. The coagulating power of the electrolytes present being reduced by dilution, by using dilute solutions we here obtain as the end-product a more highly disperse system. Thus, J. Billiter prepared a silver hydrosol (together with silver crystals) by electrolyzing 0·003 normal $AgNO_3$ solution (43). According to observations made by the writer, the formation of colloid is greater if the cathode surface is made rather small in order to raise the current density. Billiter was able to produce hydrosols of some other metals, *e.g.*, mercury, lead, by the same method.

Guided by some observations made by J. Blake concerning the pulverization of silver in the electric arc (44), the writer was able to prepare silver alcosols by the electrolysis of alcohol with silver electrodes. It has been proved by H. Nordenson that this process takes place in such a way that silver is first dissolved at the anode (in the form of some chemical compound), and is then reduced at the cathode (45). The silver cathode may in fact be replaced by a platinum cathode without affecting the production of silver colloid. This process may be given as an example of a " false " dispersion process, the colloid-producing process being in itself a condensation. Whether the reduction be purely electrochemical or caused by the hydrogen set free at the cathode is not yet decided.

There are some other phenomena connected with those just described which at first sight also seem to be dispersion processes, but which on closer inspection prove to be condensation (reduction) processes. The author observed that a silver plate submerged in water or alcohol gave rise to a silver colloid when illuminated by ultra-violet light or X-rays (46), and Margerita Traube-Mengarini found that even the boiling of silver in water produces some silver colloid (47). She also thought she had observed the production of hydrosols by boiling platinum and gold in water, but these results have not been confirmed by later investigators. In the case of silver the author found that even alcohol which had been left for some time in contact with a silver plate in absolute darkness gave some colloid when illuminated with ultra-violet light. Nordenson, who undertook a very careful examination of all these phenomena (48), has shown that silver is oxidized both by water and alcohol, and is thus dissolved (as AgOH or some organic compound). This silver solution may then be reduced by illumination (Svedberg) or by traces of reducing agents (Traube-Mengarini). The dissolution itself (oxidation process) is greatly accelerated by light, especially ultra-violet, and this must be considered as the cause of the rather rapid production of silver sol. As stated by the author, some other metals, *e.g.*, lead and copper, also give sols when illuminated in water and alcohol ; but according to Nordenson these sols contain the metal in an oxidized state. It seems that in this case, too, the oxidation process is very much increased by light, no reduction, however, taking place afterwards. Sols are therefore produced only when the oxides or hydroxides are but very slightly soluble in the dispersion medium used.

No direct dispersion of metal through light is as yet known.

By means of the reduction method we are also able to get sols of the metals of the platinum group and of mercury, bismuth, copper, tellurium and selenium. In these cases the condensation process has not been subjected to any detailed study, all the work being as yet of a preparatory nature. Some of the most interesting methods of this kind will be mentioned below.

F.C.

As has been pointed out by the writer some years ago, all reduction methods may be placed in one of the following classes, according to the manner in which the electric charges of the ions to be reduced are removed (49) :—

1. The electric charges may be transferred to hydrogen either by using elementary gaseous hydrogen or by using some suitable organic compound in the presence of water, hydrogen ions being thereby produced. The following examples illustrate this reaction :

$$(2Au\,\cdots + 6Cl') + 3H_2 = 2Au + (6H\,\cdot + 6Cl')$$

(Fulhame (50) (1794), Oberkampf (51) (1811),
Vanino (52), (1905).)

$$\begin{cases} (2Ag\,\cdot + 2OH') + H_2 = 2Ag + (2OH' + 2H\cdot) \\ 2OH' + 2H\,\cdot = 2H_2O \end{cases}$$

(Kohlschütter (53) (1908).)

$$(2Au\,\cdots + 6Cl') + 3H_2O + 3HCHO = 2Au + (6H\,\cdot + 6Cl') + 3HCOOH$$

(Zsigmondy (54) (1898).)

2. The charges may be transferred to neutral metal masses, which thereby send an equivalent quantity of metal ions into the solution, *e.g.*,

$$(4Au\,\cdots + 12Cl') + 3Sn = 4Au + (3Sn\,\cdots + 12Cl')$$

(Fischer (55) (1827).)

3. The charges may be transferred to such ions of low oxidation degree as have a tendency to pass into a higher oxidation degree, *e.g.*,

$$(2Hg\,\cdot + 2NO_3') + (Sn\,\cdot\cdot + 2NO_3) = 2Hg + (Sn\,\cdots + 4NO_3')$$

(Lottermoser (56) (1898).)

4. The charges may be neutralized by introducing negative electrons in the system (electrolysis), *e.g.*,

$$\begin{cases} (4Hg\,\cdot + 4NO_3') + 2\ominus = 4Hg + 4NO_3' \\ 4NO_3' + 4\ominus + 2H_2O = (4H\,\cdot + 4NO_3') + O_2 \end{cases}$$

(Billiter (57) (1902).)

The first and the third groups include those reduction processes that have hitherto been of the greatest importance in practice.

In the third group we have Carey Lea's method, mentioned above, for preparing silver hydrosols, and, further, Lottermoser's method. By the aid of the latter process, which uses stannous salts as a reducing agent, the hydrosols of mercury, bismuth and copper may be prepared.

In the first group are included almost all other reduction methods of importance. The reduction of silver by hydrogen (Kohlschütter), and gold by hydrogen peroxide (Stoeckl and Vanino, Doerinckel), by phosphorus (Faraday, Zsigmondy), by formaldehyde (Zsigmondy), and by hydrazine chlorhydrate (Gutbier) have already been described. Hydrazine hydrate, hydrazine chlorhydrate, phenylhydrazine chlorhydrate, and hydroxylamin chlorhydrate have, according to Gutbier, proved to be very good reducing agents. The hydrosols of the metals of the platinum group, as well as those of selenium and tellurium, may be prepared by their aid (58). Paal and his students have worked out some very efficient reduction methods (59). The alkaline salts of · protalbic and lysalbic acid are used as protective colloids. In the case of gold and silver no other reducing agent is necessary. The preparation of the hydrosols of platinum, osmium, palladium, iridium, copper, tellurium and selenium requires, however, the addition of a special reducing agent such as hydrazine hydrate, sodium amalgam, etc. Most of Paal's hydrosols can be evaporated to dryness and dissolved again in the form of sols, the protective colloids present preventing the metal particles from getting too close together.

The reduction of metals other than gold has not been known very long. Some experiments of H. Rose (1828) may be regarded as an indication of the formation of colloid silver (60), and Döbereiner (1832), perhaps, observed an unstable sol of platinum (61). The silver sub-citrate of Wöhler (62) (1839) was recognized by Newbury (1886) as a silver hydrosol (63). He remarks that the solution of Wöhler's substance, though a clear red liquid in transmittent light, appears "cloudy" in reflected light. "It seems to me highly probable," he writes, "that this red colour is caused by finely divided metallic silver." Muthmann at the same time (1887) demonstrated that the red substance, when dialyzed, did not diffuse through the parchment membrane (64).

Oxidation.

There are only two oxidation processes that are of importance for the formation of colloids, viz., the oxidation of hydrogen sulphide to sulphur (Selmi (1844) (65)), and of hydrogen selenide to selenium :

$$2H_2S + O_2 = 2S + 2H_2O$$
$$2H_2Se + O_2 = 2Se + 2H_2O$$

or

$$2H_2S + SO_2 = 3S + 2H_2O$$

In the latter case thio-acids are also formed :

$$5H_2S + 10H_2SO_3 = 3H_2S_5O_6 + 12H_2O.$$

The decomposition of thiosulphates by acids as a process furnishing colloid sulphur (Engel (1891) (66), Raffo (1908) (67)), may very well come under this heading, for the main part ($\frac{3}{4}$) of the sulphur precipitated is formed by oxidation of H_2S by SO_2 :

$$3Na_2S_2O_3 + 3H_2SO_4 = 3H_2S_2O_3 + 3Na_2SO_4$$
$$H_2S_2O_3 = S + SO_2 + H_2O$$
$$2H_2S_2O_3 + 2H_2O = 2H_2S + 2H_2SO_4$$
$$2H_2S + SO_2 = 3S + 2H_2O$$

$$\overline{3Na_2S_2O_3 + 3H_2SO_4 = 4S + 3Na_2SO_4 + 2H_2SO_4}$$
$$+ 3H_2O.$$

Odén has carefully investigated the formation of sulphur sols by the reaction between H_2S and SO_2 and by the decomposition of thiosulphates (68). The results he obtained are summed up below.

When H_2S is conducted into a solution of SO_2 in water, the amount of colloid sulphur formed and its degree of dispersion depend upon the concentration of SO_2, as is shown in the following Table. All masses are taken in grammes and refer to 100 c.c., 1·8 normal SO_2.

TABLE 8.

Concentration of SO_2.	Colloid sulphur.	"Insoluble" (non-colloid) sulphur.	Amicroscopic particles.	Nearly visible particles.	Submicroscopic particles.
1·8 normal.	8·333	0·098	0·910	4·218	3·205
1·44 ,,	9·891	0·288	0·160	2·099	7·632
0·9 ,,	13·022	0·402	0·052	0·206	12·764
0·45 ,,	1·936	14·908	Traces.	1·936	
0·225 ,,	Traces.	16·98	—	Traces.	

The amount of colloid sulphur at first increases as the concentration of SO_2 decreases, reaches a maximum, and then very rapidly decreases. The total mass of sulphur increases with the dilution of SO_2, indicating that the reaction does not follow the simple scheme

$$2H_2S + SO_2 = 3S + 2H_2O,$$

but that, according to the statements of earlier investigators (Wackenroder (69), Selmi (70), Debus (71), Spring (72), Lewes (73), Shaw (74), Hertlein (75)), it might give rise to various kinds of thio-acids and also to some sulphuric acid. At great dilutions (0·125 — 1·8 n.) the reaction will almost completely follow the simple scheme, the amount of sulphur found being 16·98 and the theoretical value

17·30. The table further shows that the *degree of dispersion of the sulphur decreases as the concentration decreases.*

As to the decomposition of sodium thiosulphate by sulphuric acid, Odén made the following observations: The formation of colloid sulphur decreases as the concentrations of the reacting components decrease, and decreases also, but only a little, with lowering of temperature.

TABLE 9.

30 c.c. 3-normal $Na_2S_2O_3$; 10 c.c. concentrated H_2SO_4.

Water. Cubic centimetres.	Colloid sulphur. Grammes.	Insoluble sulphur. Grammes.	Small particles. Grammes.	Large particles. Grammes.
0	1·691	1·031	0·910	0·781
5	1·353	1·365	0·022	1·331
10	1·273	1·282	Traces.	1·273
20	1·070	1·463	Traces.	1·070
30	0·384	2·123	—	0·384
50	0·059	2·439	—	0·059

The experiments tabulated above (Table 9) were carried out in the following manner: 30 c.c. of 3-normal $Na_2S_2O_3$ solution were mixed with various quantities of water, and then 10 c.c. concentrated sulphuric acid were added. As the concentration of $Na_2O_2S_3$ diminishes, not only does the quantity of colloid sulphur decrease, but also *the degree of dispersion* of the system. Some other experiments showed that a dilution of the sulphuric acid had an analogous effect on the formation of colloid sulphur.

In practice it is advisable not to choose too high a temperature, for the higher the temperature the stronger is the irreversible coagulating power of the cations present, viz., the sodium ions. It has also proved advantageous to use rather small quantities

of solutions, 100 c c. or so. After the formation of
the colloid sulphur the reaction mixture should be
immediately coagulated with pure sodium chloride
solution and the precipitate separated from the
liquid by centrifuging.   The bulk of the deposit dissolves in water, forming a sulphur hydrosol.   The
residue, consisting of " insoluble " sulphur, is removed
by centrifuging or by sedimentation.   By once more
adding sodium chloride solution and centrifuging, the
sulphur may be purified.   The colloid sulphur contained in the reacting mixtures from $2H_2S + SO_2$
may be freed from impurities in the same way.

Sulphur hydrosols obtained by this or by the other
methods are built up of particles of various size from
a few $\mu\mu$ to some hundreds of $\mu\mu$.   Odén has worked
out a very ingenious method of dividing the original
polydisperse sol into a series of sols with particles
of almost equal size, i.e., into a series of monodisperse
sols.   When dealing with the polydisperse sulphur
sols he observed that the small particles were less
sensitive to coagulating agents than the larger ones,
i.e., by slowly adding a salt solution the larger
particles were first precipitated.   Thus it should be
possible to fractionate the sulphur sol by means of a
reversibly coagulating salt.   Odén used sodium
chloride.   In Table 10 such a series of sols obtained by
Odén is reviewed.

The concentration necessary for coagulating a
sulphur sol, i.e., the precipitation value, varies with
the temperature.   The higher the temperature, the
higher is the precipitation value.   At a given salt
concentration the temperature at which coagulation
sets in is higher for the larger particles.   Thus on
slowly cooling a polydisperse sulphur sol, the greater
particles will be first precipitated, then the particles
that are a little smaller, and so on.   According to
Odén, a method for separating the particles of various
size may be founded on this phenomenon.

The removal of the electrolyte used for the purifying and fractionating of the sulphur colloid is carried out in the following manner. The main part of the electrolyte is removed by cooling the concentrated sol to about $-10°$, when a fairly salt-free soluble coagulum is deposited. A very efficient purification may then, according to Odén, be attained by electro-

TABLE 10.

The sulphur sol		Ultra-microscopic characteristics.
is not coagulated	is coagulated	
by NaCl of the following concentration in normality:		
0·25	∞	Faint amicroscopic light-cone, no submicrons.
0·20	0·25	Clearly visible amicroscopic light-cone, no submicrons.
0·16	0·20	Strong amicroscopic light-cone, no submicrons.
0·13	0·16	Particles just visible (about 25 $\mu\mu$ in diameter).
0·10	0·13	No amicroscopic light-cone, diameter of particles, 90 $\mu\mu$.
0·07	0·10	No amicroscopic light-cone, diameter of particles, 140 $\mu\mu$.
0	0·07	No amicroscopic light-cone, diameter of particles, 210 $\mu\mu$.

lysing the sol in an apparatus provided with suitable diaphragms.

The oxidation of hydrogen selenide to selenium hydrosol is of less importance and has not yet been sufficiently studied.

A curious case of electrolytic pulverization studied by E. Müller and his students, and hitherto looked upon as a dispersion process, may most probably be regarded as an oxidation process (76). If a platinum plate is covered to some extent with sulphur and used as a cathode in pure water, colloid sulphur is produced at the contact surface between the sulphur and the platinum. Selenium and tellurium show analogous phenomena. The explanation is probably that hydrogen sulphide is first formed by a reaction between the electrolytically produced hydrogen and the sulphur, and that this H_2S is then oxidized by the oxygen dissolved in the water. Another explanation would be that a very unstable hydrogen persulphide (H_2S_2) is formed at the cathode and that it dissociates into H_2S and colloid sulphur. In this case the process should be included in the following group (dissociation processes).

The formation of sulphur hydrosols by oxidation of hydrogen sulphide water may probably be one of the colloid formation processes first observed. The gradual clouding of the natural sulphur waters has long been known. In fact, our knowledge of it is perhaps of the same date as our acquaintance with those waters. Scheele (77) (about 1770), Bergman (78) (1782), Le Veillard (79) (1789), Berthollet (80) (1798), Berzelius (81) (1808) and Döbereiner (82) (1813) mention such reactions in their treatises. Berzelius writes as follows : " In water it (H_2S) dissolves abundantly . . . if the water contain atmospheric air some part of the air is destroyed, the hydrogen being oxydized to water and the sulphur set free, on which the water gets a milky appearance." Wackenroder (83) (1846) studied the turbid liquid obtained by passing H_2S through an aqueous solution of SO_2, and Selmi (84) (1844–5) made this liquid the subject of a close examination that brought him to a very clear and modern view of the form of existence of the sulphur in it and its colloid chemical reactions. He recognized the connections between such products as the disperse systems of Prussian blue, As_2S_3, casein, albumin,

Wackenroder's liquid, etc., and called them pseudo-solutions: "*Il resulte, en outre, que le soufre émulsionnable présente des phénomènes analogues à ceux qui s'observent dans beaucoup d'autres corps qui jouissent de la propriété de se disperser et se diviser dans un liquide, sans toutefois s'y dissoudre absolument, tels que le savon, l'amidon et le bleu de Prusse. . . .* Some years later (1888) Debus (85) expresses a similar opinion : "If we look back on the properties of the sulphur as it is contained in solution in Wackenroder's liquid, and can be obtained from it by partial evaporation, we find that it possesses all the properties which Graham describes as characteristic of the colloids."

" The sulphur dissolved in Wackenroder's solution does not diffuse through porous clay or parchment. It is held in solution by very feeble forces. Slow and gradual separation takes place when its solutions are kept for some time, or complete precipitation if apparently inert substances, such as sodium chloride, charcoal powder, or basic sulphate, are added. The unstable condition of its molecules, their slow change into other modifications, and finally its gummy, sticky condition remind one of the colloids."

Dissociation.

The formation of disperse systems by dissociation is as yet but very imperfectly known. Some processes will be treated here which are probably to be referred to this class.

As already mentioned above, some ($\frac{1}{4}$) of the colloid sulphur formed by the action of acids upon thiosulphates is derived from a dissociation of thioic acid :

$$H_2S_2O_3 = S + SO_2 + H_2O.$$

Some polysulphides also produce colloid sulphur on dissociating.

Wa. Ostwald observed that a solution of nickel carbonyl in benzene when boiled gives rise to a nickel benzosol (86). The process is no doubt to be regarded as a dissociation, viz. :

$$Ni(CO)_4 \rightarrow Ni + 4CO.$$

All organic compounds dissociate at high temperatures, and may under suitable conditions give rise to disperse systems of carbon. The Acheson graphite used in lubrication is manufactured by treating carbon dust formed in the carborundum furnaces with gallotannic acid and water (87).

Much more important is the dissociation of salts, especially metal halides, by which process the metal under suitable conditions may be deposited in highly disperse form. Among this group of phenomena may be included the darkening of the silver halides in the light. According to R. Lorenz, it is possible to follow the formation and growth of the silver particles in pure silver bromide by means of the ultra-microscope (88). In the optically empty mass there first appears an amicroscopic light-cone, which gradually disintegrates into submicroscopic particles. As has been shown by R. Lorenz and his students, many metal halides dissociate spontaneously, even in the dark, into metal and halide, $e.g.$, $PbCl_2$, $TlCl$, $TlBr$, $AgCl$, $AgBr$, and this process takes place both in the fused salts and in solid crystals. Of course the degree of dissociation is rather small. Optically empty systems of these salts exist only in the presence of some excess of halide. As an example, the preparation of optically empty $PbCl_2$ will be described. About 100 gm. of commercial lead chloride is melted in a tube of hard glass placed within an electric resistance furnace and treated for one to two hours with a mixture of dry hydrochloric and chlorine gas. Then the glass tube is taken out of the furnace and cooled. The congealed mass consists of pure optically empty crystals of lead chloride. If a piece of metallic lead is introduced into a pure fused specimen of $PbCl_2$ of this sort there occurs a kind of pulverization of the metal, a brownish black lead fog emanating from it. This phenomenon may perhaps be explained in the following way. By the presence of the metallic lead the equilibrium in the melted salt is disturbed and the dissociation of the halide into metal and chlorine is increased. If such a black fused mixture is cooled and then put to an ultra-microscopic test, it will prove to contain numerous metal particles, some of which are amicroscopic and others submicroscopic. The system is therefore to be regarded as a colloid solution of metal in salt. R. Lorenz has adopted the name " pyrosol " for such systems.

This " metal pulverization " in fused salts was first observed in the electrolysis of such systems and regarded as a kind of electric cathode pulverization (Faraday, Bunsen). The earlier investigators did not, however, pay attention to the fact that all salts, even " dry " ones, always contain a little water that cannot be removed by heating only. For a halide it is necessary to heat the salt in a current of HCl at a slowly rising temperature in order to get rid of the water and avoid hydrolysis. If this precaution is not taken, oxides and oxychlorides will be formed during the electrolysis, and the metal fog phenomenon cannot be clearly observed, but appears as part of the general clouding of the electrolyte.

Another very interesting phenomenon, observed by H. Siedentopf, may perhaps be of an analogous nature (89). He found that dry crystals of rock salt heated with sodium vapour *in vacuo* assumed a blue coloration and became quite like the natural blue rock salt sometimes found in salt mines. When examined in the ultra-microscope the blue salt, the artificial as well as the natural variety, proved to contain numerous metallic particles, arranged in the directions of cleavage of the crystal. The explanation may be that the sodium vapour penetrating into the fine clefts of the crystal disturbs the equilibrium of the halide and causes some dissociation of it and formation of sodium colloid by a condensation process. Obviously there is also another explanation—adopted by Siedentopf—viz., that the sodium colloid is produced directly from the sodium vapour by condensation in the fine clefts of the crystal. Now blue rock salt may also be prepared in another manner, viz., by exposing ordinary rock salt to cathode or radium rays. In this case the mechanism of the process must of course be a dissociation of $NaCl$ into $Na + Cl$. The identity of the products obtained by this method and by the treating of rock salt with sodium vapour may be interpreted in favour of the opinion held by the writer.

Many other forms of coloration caused by cathode and radium rays in various substances should, according to Doelter, be regarded as colloid colours (90). The chemical reactions, dissociations or double decompositions to which the substances may be subjected are as yet almost completely unknown.

Double Decomposition.

A great many double decomposition reactions give rise to disperse systems.

The cases of most interest are :

1. Formation of *oxide* sols by
    (a) Hydrolysis.
    (b) Precipitation with alkalis.
    (c) Decomposition of salts with acids.

2. Formation of *sulphide* sols by
    (a) Precipitation with hydrogen sulphide.
    (b) Decomposition of sulpho-salts.

3. Formation of *salt* sols by precipitation with easily soluble
   - (*a*) Halides.
   - (*b*) Sulphates.
   - (*c*) Chromates.
   - (*d*) Phosphates.
   - (*e*) Ferro- and ferri-cyanides.

As to the question of the relation between the experimental conditions and the degree of dispersion of the system formed, a great many experiments have been carried out with various double decomposition reactions in order to settle this matter. P. P. v. Weimarn, who has devoted a great deal of work to this subject (91), pronounces the opinion that as the concentration of the reacting substances decreases, the degree of dispersion—measured a quarter to half an hour after the reaction—first decreases and then increases again. When measured about a month after the reaction the degree of dispersion is supposed always to rise with concentration. This view v. Weimarn has tried to maintain, especially by his investigations on the formation of $BaSO_4$ from $MnSO_4 + Ba(SCN)_2$.

Recent investigations by Odén have shown that the degree of dispersion always diminishes as the concentration decreases (92). By means of a special apparatus he was able to measure the distribution of the various sizes of particles in $BaSO_4$—suspensions produced when, under various conditions, he mixed a solution of barium ions, *e.g.*, $Ba(SCN)_2$, with a solution of sulphate ions, *e.g.*, $(NH_4)_2SO_4$. The formation of secondary particles, *i.e.*, aggregates of primary particles, easily misleads the investigator. Odén found that secondary particles are very often formed when the size of the particle is small. Above 100 $\mu\mu$ scarcely any are formed, but below 20 $\mu\mu$ one nearly always gets secondary particles if no special precautions are taken, *e.g.*, the addition of citrate, in order to prevent aggregation and to cause such aggregates as may have been formed owing to local

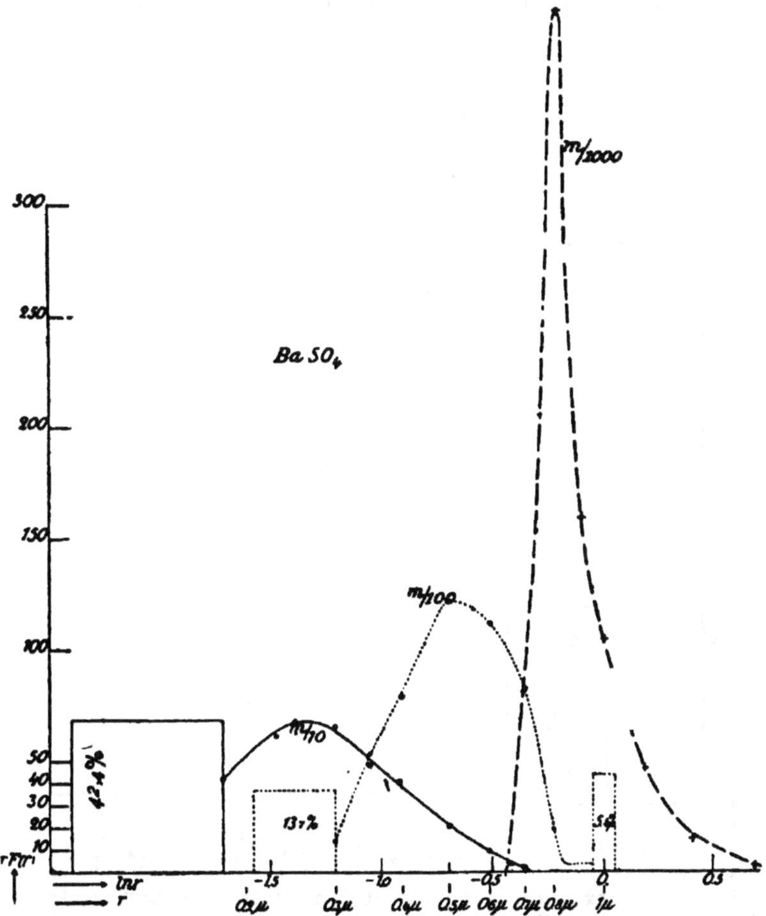

FIG. 18.—Variation of degree of dispersion, as represented by the distribution curve, with concentration of reacting ions. (According to Odén.)

high concentration of electrolytes to redissolve into primary particles. The chemical reaction, being a pure ionic reaction, is supposed to take place exceedingly fast, and the supersaturation immediately before condensation should therefore be equal to the ratio between the total concentration of $BaSO_4$ and the solubility of $BaSO_4$. Thus it is in agreement with the result obtained for condensation in gases that

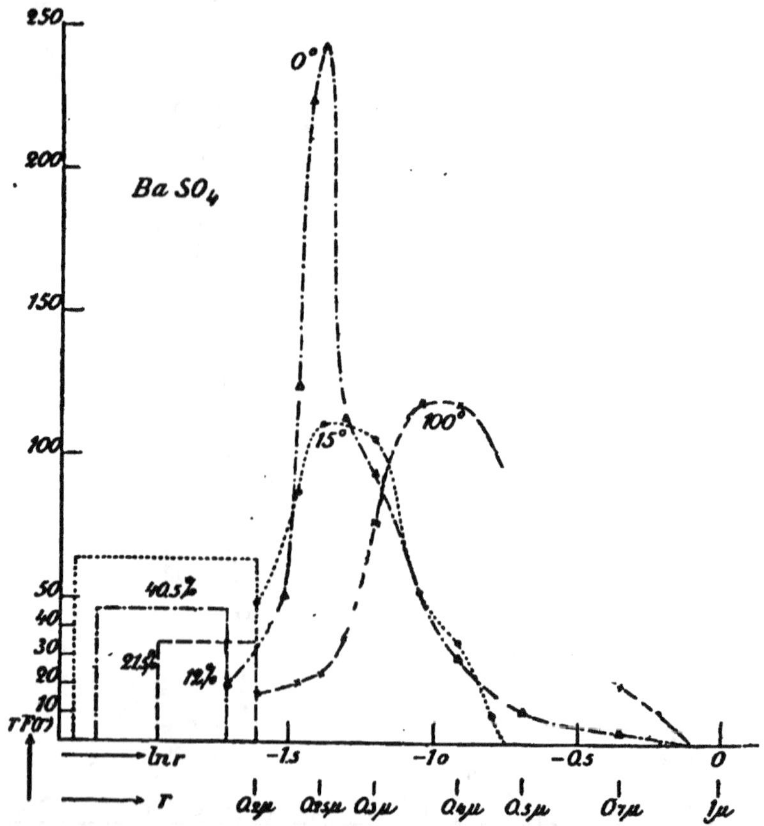

FIG. 19.—Variation of degree of dispersion with temperature during the reaction. (According to Odén.)

the degree of dispersion increases as the concentration rises. The production of nuclei seems to be almost exclusively spontaneous. Odén found that particles of $BaSO_4$ added to one of the reaction components before the reaction have little or no influence on the degree of dispersion of the system formed. In

TABLE II.

Experiments on the relation between the degree of dispersion, as represented by the distribution curve, and the concentration of the reacting ions, *i.e.*, the degree of supersaturation.

	$F(r)$.		
r.	Molar concentration of $BaSO_4$-ion at the moment of reaction.		
	0·1	0·01.	0·001.
2·0	—	—	1·35
1·5	—	—	9·9
1·2	—	0	38·9
1·0	—	4·6	105·0
0·9	—	0	178
0·8	—	23·9	485
0·75	0	72·5	275
0·70	2·7	118	
0·60	16·0	187	
0·55	—	218	
0·50	42·0	244	
0·46	—	224	
0·40	102	198	
0·37	—	—	
0·35	137	151	
0·33	161	—	
0·31	194	—	
0·30	219	47·0	
0·27	255		
0·25	273		
0·23	268		
0·20	258		
0·18	233		
Coarse material.	—	$\int_{0·9}^{1·2} F(r)dr = 5·4$ per cent.	—
Fine-grained residue.	$\int_{0}^{0·18} F(r)dr = 72·4$ per cent.	$\int_{0}^{0·30} F(r)dr = 13·7$ per cent.	$\int_{0·65}^{0·75} F(r)dr = 17$ per cent.

Table 11 and Fig. 18 a few of Odén's most characteristic experimental series are presented.

Here r denotes the radius of the particles in μ (or, properly, the radius of a sphere of the same material sinking with the same velocity in the same fluid).

$F(r)$ the functional relation between the percentage mass of particles and the radius, and

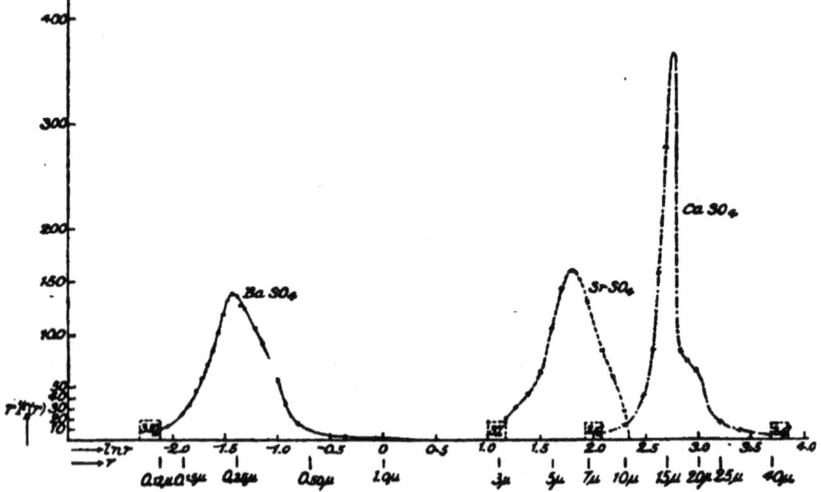

FIG. 20.—Variation of degree of dispersion with solubility of the disperse phase formed.   (According to Odén.)

$F(r)dr$ the percentage mass of particles in the radius interval dr.

In the figures the lnr are plotted as abscissæ against the $rF(r)$ as ordinates in order to have a suitable form of graphic representation.

The temperature of the reacting mixture influences the degree of dispersion of the system produced. Odén found the following values (Table 12) (Fig. 19) for the reaction products of 0·2 molar solutions of $Ba(SCN)_2$ and $(NH_4)_2SO_4$ at 0°, 15° and 100°.

Thus the degree of dispersion becomes lower as the temperature rises, a fact that is very probably due to the increased solubility of the disperse phase at higher temperatures.

TABLE 12.

	$F(r)$.		
	0°	15°	100°
1·0	0	—	0
0·8	—	—	14·0
0·7	6·0	—	28·7
0·6	11·6	0	61·2
0·55	—	—	—
0·50	21·6	—	164
0·45	—	21·3	224
0·40	74·0	88·3	296
0·35	150	146	338
0·33	—	200	329
0·32	204	—	—
0·30	314	353	256
0·27	419	437	135
0·25	972	444	96·5
0·24	934	—	—
0·23	540	378	91·3
0·22	229	—	—
0·20	174	241	84·5
0·18	165		
0·17			
Fine-grained residue.	$\int_0^{0·18} F(r)dr = 21·5$ per cent.	$\int_0^{0·20} F(r)dr = 40·4$ per cent.	$\int_0^{0·20} F(r)dr = 12$ per cent.

Odén compared the degree of dispersion of systems of $BaSO_4$, $SrSO_4$ and $CaSO_4$ produced by mixing 0·2 molar solutions of the nitrates with 0·2 molar solutions of ammonium sulphate (Table 13) (Fig. 20).

TABLE 13.

BaSO$_4$.		SrSO$_4$.		CaSO$_4$.	
r.	$F(r)$.	r.	$F(r)$.	r.	$F(r)$.
1·0	1·3	10	2·74	40	0·10
0·7	4·6	9	6·67	30	0·27
0·5	16·4	8	10·6	25	0·62
0·45	36·0	7	18·6	20	3·37
0·40	87·2	6	27·0	18	4·16
0·37	154	5·5	26·0	17	4·95
0·35	215	5·0	21·4	16	23·1
0·32	287	4·5	14·4	15	18·6
0·30	355	4·0	11·0	14	11·4
0·27	465	3·5	8·80	13	6·61
0·26	494	3·2	6·44	12	3·59
0·25	548	—	—	10	1·37
0·24	579	—	—	8	0·84
0·23	578				
0·22	545				
0·21	488				
0·20	429				
0·19	379				
0·18	327				
0·17	280				
0·16	209				
0·15	167				
0·13	102				
0·12	83·5				
		Coarse material.	$\int_{10}^{\infty} F(r)\,dr = 0\cdot5$ p.c.	Coarse material.	$\int_{40}^{\infty} F(r)\,dr = 2\cdot5$ per cent.
Fine-grained residue.	0·12 $\int_{0} F(r)\,dr = 3\cdot9$ per cent.	Fine-grained residue.	3·2 $\int_{0} F(r)\,dr = 3$ per cent.	Fine-grained residue.	8 $\int_{0} F(r)\,dr = 2\cdot8$ per cent.

With regard to the secondary and tertiary degree
of dispersion studied by Odén in the case of BaSO$_4$,
reference will be made to these investigations in a

subsequent monograph dealing with the changes of state in colloids.

In cases when the chemical reaction proceeds slowly, *e.g.*, in the formation of colloid As_2S_3 from As_2O_3-solution by the action of H_2S or during hydrolysis of $FeCl_3$, the degree of dispersion decreases as the concentration increases, as was the case with the reduction of $HAuCl_4$. It is not yet known, however, to what extent the formation of secondary particles, *i.e.*, aggregates, may be responsible for the effect observed.

Berzelius had already observed that the reaction

$$As_2O_3 + 3H_2S = As_2S_3 + 3H_2O$$

gave rise to a yellow solution of As_2S_3, and he remarks that " this solution probably ought to be regarded more as a suspension of transparent particles " (93). Schulze found that by means of the said method systems of various properties can be obtained according to the concentrations of As_2O_3 at which the reaction takes place. He writes as follows : " It is very remarkable that the fluids which are obtained by diluting the more concentrated ones do not in all respects resemble the directly made solutions of the same degree of concentration. In transparency the former are very inferior to the latter, and they show in reflected light a more or less pure yellow colour in contradistinction to the rich yellow colour of the solutions directly made " (94).

A little later Picton and Linder (95) prepared As_2S_3-sols by various double decomposition methods, and they notice, a point that Schulze had overlooked, that the properties of these " pseudo-solutions " depend on the size of the particles of which they are built up. The As_2S_3-sol that contained the greatest particles (just visible in a microscope), the " α-solution " of Linder and Picton, was prepared by mixing arsenical tartrate solution with hydrogen sulphide water. The "β-solution," obtained by mixing sodium arsenite and hydrogen sulphide water, could not be resolved with the microscope, and "presented the appearance of a perfectly homogeneous liquid." Still it showed no trace of diffusion. The "γ-solution, prepared by mixing concentrated As_2O_3-solution, about 9·5 per cent., with hydrogen sulphide water, resembled the β-solution, but showed a slight diffusion. Yet it was not filtrable. Finally the "δ-solution," obtained by the same reaction as the γ-solution, but from a more dilute (about 2 per cent.) As_2O_3-solution, was diffusible as well as filtrable. It still gave, however, the Tyndall light-cone. Linder and Picton remark that the δ-sol must be looked upon as containing particles of smaller size than the γ-sol. Some investigations of the writer concerning the light absorption in As_2S_3-sols show that the degree of dispersion rises more and more as the dilution of As_2O_3 is increased (96). He studied dilutions up to $1 \cdot 10^{-7}$ normal. This result has been confirmed by recent experiments of G. Börjeson, who succeeded in determining the absolute size of the particles in a series of As_2S_3-sols obtained from As_2O_3 solutions of various concentrations (97). In Table 14 some of his measurements are given :

TABLE 14.

Concentration of As_2O_3.	Radius of particles of As_2S_3.
$1 \cdot 10^{-2}$ normal.	39 $\mu\mu$
$5 \cdot 10^{-4}$,,	16 $\mu\mu$
$1 \cdot 10^{-4}$,,	11 $\mu\mu$

Some other processes by which sulphide sols may be obtained will also be mentioned. Reactions of the type where only slightly electrolytic dissociated substances are formed have, besides the case already mentioned, been used also in the following cases. Copper and zinc sulphide hydrosols were prepared by Linder and Picton by treating the hydrates suspended in water with hydrogen sulphide (98). Lottermoser treated mercury cyanide, glycocol copper, and copper acetoacetic ester with hydrogen sulphide and obtained sulphide sols of those metals (99). He even succeeded in carrying out the reaction in organic solvents, *e.g.*, alcohol and ether, and thus obtained sulphide organosols.

Reactions which give rise to strongly dissociated products may be used for the preparation of sulphide sols in any of the following ways, viz.: 1. By operating in highly diluted solution. 2. By adding a protective colloid. 3. By removing the electrolytes or replacing the ions present by more suitable, *i.e.*, less coagulating, ions. Process 1 was first observed by Berzelius (100) and by Schulze (101), and later on practised by Winssinger (102). Process 2 has been used by many investigators. Paal dissolved protalbic or lysalbic silver in ammonium sulphide, and thus obtained colloid silver sulphide protected by the ammonium salt of the protalbic or lysalbic acid (103). After dialyzing, the sol was precipitated with alcohol and the precipitate dried. This protected colloid silver sulphide dissolves easily in water, forming a hydrosol again. Process 3 was also observed by Berzelius (104). Spring used it for the preparation of copper sulphide sol (105). He washed copper sulphide coagulum with H_2S-water.

Hydrolysis, *i.e.*, the decomposition of a compound by water, is a reaction of great interest for colloid chemistry. It may be regarded as a double decomposition reaction, viz.,

$$MeAc + H_2O \rightleftarrows MeOH + HAc,$$

where Me stands for a metal atom, and Ac for an acid group.

In many cases it takes considerable time to reach equilibrium. Goodwin (106), who studied the hydrolysis of ferric chloride, has suggested that, in such cases, first a rapid reaction of the kind

$$Fe^{\cdots} + H_2O = FeOH^{\cdot\cdot} + H^{\cdot}$$

takes place, and after that a slow formation of Fe_2O_3. This product then condenses to a Fe_2O_3 —or $Fe(OH)_3$—sol. The hydrolytic equilibrium varies with the dilution. At 25° C., Goodwin found the following values (Table 15) :— .

TABLE 15.

Concentration mol/lit.	Degree of hydrolysis in percentage.
0·45	2
0·225	11
0·090	37
0·045	53
0·0225	67
0·0090	84
0·0045	91

Thus there is practically no hydrolysis above the concentration $5 \cdot 10^{-1}$ mol/lit, and below $3 \cdot 10^{-3}$ there is almost total hydrolysis. The velocity of the hydrolysis differs considerably for various degrees of temperature and dilution. It increases as the temperature and the dilution increase, and is likewise increased by insolation. At 25° C., Goodwin found that for the concentration $1 \cdot 10^{-4}$ equilibrium was practically attained in three hours, whereas a week was needed when the concentration was $6 \cdot 10^{-4}$. The writer (107) carried out a series of measurements on the light absorption in hydrosols of Fe_2O_3 prepared by hydrolysis of $FeCl_3$ at various dilutions, from $1 \cdot 10^{-3}$ to $1 \cdot 10^{-7}$. He found that the absorption per unit mass of Fe_2O_3 first increases, and, after reaching a maximum, decreases again, just as in the case of other series of sols with an increasing degree of dispersion. Some ultra-microscopic observations by W. Biltz support the view that, when a disperse system is formed by hydrolysis, the degree of dispersion increases as the dilution increases (108).

Gay-Lussac (109) (1810) and Berzelius (110) (1833) were the first investigators to mention the formation of peculiar "soluble" forms of substances by hydrolysis. Berzelius describes the preparation of "b-silicic acid," *i.e.*, the hydrosol of SiO_2, thus : " In its purest state it is formed by oxidation of silicon sulphide at the expense of water ; hydrogen sulphide is set free, and the b-silicic acid dissolves in the water. In concentrated form the solution soon coagulates to a jelly-like mass." The formation of " pseudo-solutions " by hydrolysis of acetates was studied by Crum (111) (1853), Péan de Saint-Gilles (112) (1855), and also by Graham (113) (1861) in his fundamental series of colloid investigations. Graham carried out the hydrolysis in a dialyzer, and thus accelerated the reaction by removing the free acid. Later investigators have followed him in that path. In the second half of the nineteenth century a great many experiments concerning the preparation of hydrosols by hydrolysis have been carried out on various salts, and on other compounds too. A method employed by Grimaux is especially interesting on account of the absence of inorganic products except the colloids (114). He prepared Fe_2O_3 hydrosol by mixing ferriethylate with water, and SiO_2 hydrosol by heating an aqueous solution of the methylester of silicic acid. The methylalcohol contained in the silicic acid hydrosol thus obtained may be driven off by boiling.

A great many other double decomposition reactions have been used for the preparation of disperse systems. Among these are some of the classical procedures of Graham, first described in his famous paper, "Liquid Diffusion applied to Analysis," of 1861. He prepared "soluble silicic acid" by decomposing silicate of soda with hydrochloric acid and dialyzing for 24 hours. Many oxides were precipitated from their salts as coagula, and then peptized with some suitable salt and dialyzed, $e.g.$, Al_2O_3 with $AlCl_3$, Fe_2O_3 with $FeCl_3$, Cr_2O_3 with $CrCl_3$, SnO_2 with $SnCl_4$, etc.

Lottermoser studied the formation of silver halides in dilute solution (115). If $n/10AgNO_3$ is slowly poured into $n/10KJ$, an AgJ-hydrosol is formed and remains stable until no excess of KJ is present, when coagulation takes place. Inversely, if $n/10KJ$ is poured into $n/10AgNO_3$, an AgJ-hydrosol is likewise formed, and remains stable until all excess of $AgNO_3$ is removed. The two forms of AgJ-hydrosols thus obtained carry electric charges of contrary signs, the former being negative and the latter positive.

The hydrosols of the ferrocyanides can be prepared, according to Zsigmondy (116), in an analogous way, viz., by pouring the dilute metal salt solution into the dilute solution of potassium ferrocyanide, or inversely, taking care that there should be excess of the solution reacted upon when the operation is finished.

Many substances not to be obtained as hydrosols because of their great solubility in water may be prepared as organosols. Some rather interesting methods of this kind have been worked out by Paal (117). Michael had observed (118) that chloracetic ester, when brought into reaction with sodium malonester, acetoacetic ester and their simple alkyl substitution products dissolved in benzene gave rise to a yellowish, slightly opalescent liquid. As no sodium chloride was deposited, Michael believed that some addition-product, *e.g.*, $C_{11}H_{18}O_6ClNa$, had been formed. Paal now showed that the sodium chloride existed free in the liquid in the form of a colloid. It could be precipitated with petroleum ether as a gel and redissolved in benzene as an almost pure NaCl-sol, protected by a trace of some high molecular organic substance formed as by-product in the reaction. Paal and his students also obtained the organosols of NaBr and NaJ by analogous methods.

DISPERSION PROCESSES.

As our knowledge of the mechanism of the formation of disperse systems has increased, an increasing number of those processes formerly regarded as dispersion processes have proved to be in reality condensation phenomena, *e.g.*, the formation of colloids by means of the electric arc, by electrolysis, by ultra-violet light, by boiling, etc. As pure dispersion phenomena there only remain a few processes. Three groups may be distinguished, viz. :

      1. Partial dissolution.
      2. Grinding.
      3. Emulsification.

The formation of disperse systems by partial dissolution or the raising of the degree of dispersion of a low disperse system by the same means has been studied by P. P. v. Weimarn (119). As has already been mentioned (p. 55), a highly disperse sulphur alcosol prepared by the rapid cooling of a solution of sulphur in alcohol, when warmed, has its degree of dispersion first lowered in consequence of the growth of the larger particles at the cost of the smaller ones, and then raised in consequence of the resolution of the particles in the dispersion medium. If tellurium is dissolved in potassium hydroxide solution, and the solution is then diluted (*e.g.*, 5 c.c. per 1,000 c.c. H_2O), a coarse suspension of tellurium is obtained.   If air or oxygen is passed through the liquid the tellurium particles are oxidized and partly dissolved, most probably because of the formation of potassium tellurate.   Hence the degree of dispersion increases (P. P. v. Weimarn).   Starting with a pure solution of potassium tellurate, we may, inversely, as was already shown by Berzelius (120) (1834), precipitate the tellurium in the form of fine particles by passing oxygen through it.   When further treated with oxygen these particles will be partially oxidized and redissolved, $i.e.$, the degree of dispersion is diminished. Thus in this case we get by the same means, viz., by treating with oxygen, first a condensation process— formation of colloid Te by oxidation of K_2Te:

$$K_2Te + O + H_2O = Te + 2KOH;$$

and then a dispersion process, $i.e.$, partial dissolution of the Te-particles according to the reaction :

$$Te + 2KOH + O_2 = K_2TeO_3 + H_2O.$$

Those processes have not yet become of any practical importance for the preparation of colloid solutions.

As stated above, the so-called peptization processes are in general to be considered as reversible coagulations.   They are not real dispersion processes, the degree of dispersion not being altered by the peptization, but only the mutual distances of the particles.   There may, however, exist peptizations where a partial dissolution of the particles is of a certain importance; thus, for instance, according to P. P. v. Weimarn (121), the peptization of Al_2O_3 by alkalis (formation of aluminate) and of SiO_2 by alkalis (formation of silicate), etc.

An intermediate position is occupied by the colloidation methods of Wedekind (122) and Kužel (123). The mechanism of these processes is not yet quite clear, but it may most probably consist in a sort of combination of a real dispersion process and an ordinary peptization. According to Wedekind, metallic zirconium is prepared by the reduction of some suitable zirconium compound, *e.g.*, zirconium dioxide with magnesium or zirconium potassium fluoride with potassium, and the product obtained is treated with hydrochloric acid. If the mass is then washed with water, part of the zirconium goes into solution as a colloid. The reduction product may again be treated with acid and it will, when washed, give off a new portion of zirconium colloid. Kužel's method is carried out in the following way. The metal to be brought into the colloid state, *e.g.*, tungsten, molybdenum, silicon, zirconium, titanium, is first pulverized very finely by grinding, is then treated alternately with acid and alkali, and washed with water between these treatments. No doubt the colloidation depends here to some extent on a real dissolution of the particles by the acid and alkali, but in the opinion of the author it may also to a considerable extent be the result of an ordinary peptization, *i.e.*, a separation of the aggregated particles. In the case of pure mechanical grinding it is generally possible, as will be shown later on, to get colloids if the particles are only prevented from aggregating too closely together. This fact is obviously in favour of the view just put forth, that the chemical reagents in Wedekind's and Kužel's methods only serve to a great extent to bring about the loosening of the particles from one another. Kužel's colloids were used in the manufacture of filaments for electric incandescent lamps. The sol was coagulated with some suitable electrolyte, and the plastic mass obtained pressed through fine holes. The wire thus formed was then heated so as to get the particles to sinter together to a solid wire.

It may be of interest to note that Wedekind's method goes back to some old observations made by Davy in 1808 (124) and by Berzelius in 1824 (125). Davy found that boron, prepared by reduction of boric acid with potassium, is redissolved when washed with water : " The solutions obtained, when passing through a filter, had a faint olive tint, and contained sub-borate of potash and potash. In cases when, instead of water, a weak solution of muriatic acid was used for separating the saline matter from the inflammable matter, the fluid came through the filter colourless."

The preparation of disperse systems by means of purely mechanical grinding is, as yet, only very little studied. It seems, however, that the view held by earlier investigators, that only rather coarse disperse systems could be obtained in this manner, cannot be maintained. On the contrary, recent work points to the conclusion that, under suitable conditions, it will generally be possible to produce rather highly disperse systems by purely mechanical subdivision. On grinding a substance there are most probably formed, besides the coarse particles, very fine ones as well ; but as the grinding goes on these coalesce and form aggregates, which appear as coarse particles. As in the case of many chemical colloidation processes, a secondary degree of dispersion is taken for the primary one. If the aggregation is prevented, we get the primary structure, *i.e.*, highly disperse systems.

P. P. v. Weimarn suggested the use of some indifferent solid dilution matter, to be mixed during the grinding with the substance to be subdivided (126). If the dilution matter and the substance be chosen so as to allow the former to be dissolved while leaving the particles of the substance unaffected when put into some liquid dispersion medium, it will be possible to obtain a colloid solution of the latter. He pointed out further that, by means of successive dilution and grinding with the solid dilution matter, it should be possible to prepare a series of colloids with successively increasing degrees of dispersion. N. Pihlblad has shown this to be experimentally realizable (127). He ground sulphur with urea in an agate mortar ; first 0·1 gm. S + 1 gm. urea, then 0·1 gm. of this mixture + 1 gm. urea, and so on. On dissolving the ground products in water, he obtained a series of sulphur hydrosols with increasing degree of dispersion. Similar experiences were made when grinding in the same way the dye-stuff " anilinblau 2 B " (from A.G.F.A., Berlin), which is insoluble in water. A. L. Stein, a student of v. Weimarn (128), is said to have carried out many such experiments, but as yet we are without any detailed information regarding the nature of the dilution matter, etc.

G. Wegelin (129) has succeeded in preparing rather highly disperse systems by simply grinding the pure substances with or without water, *e.g.*, silicon, antimony, tungstic acid, titanic acid, molybdic acid, melted vanadic acid, vanadic trioxide. On the other hand, he had no success with copper, bismuth, tellurium, selenium, sulphur, graphite, CuO, PbO_2, ZnO, CoO, Fe_2O_3, CaF_2, violet chromic chloride. We may suspect, however, that, especially in the case of the very easily dispersed vanadic acid, some chemical reaction plays a part in the process. The question deserves further examination (130).

The formation of disperse systems by emulsification is important, both from a theoretical and from a practical point of view. The investigations by I. Nordlund (131) have shown that in the case of emulsification we have to distinguish between two different processes, viz. :—

1. Crushing of drops (dispersion process).
2. Formation of lamellæ (dispersion process) and

bursting of the lamellæ, small drops being thereby produced (condensation process).

When a disperse system is prepared by the shaking up of two non-miscible liquids whose interfacial tension is high, it is mainly process 2 that occurs.

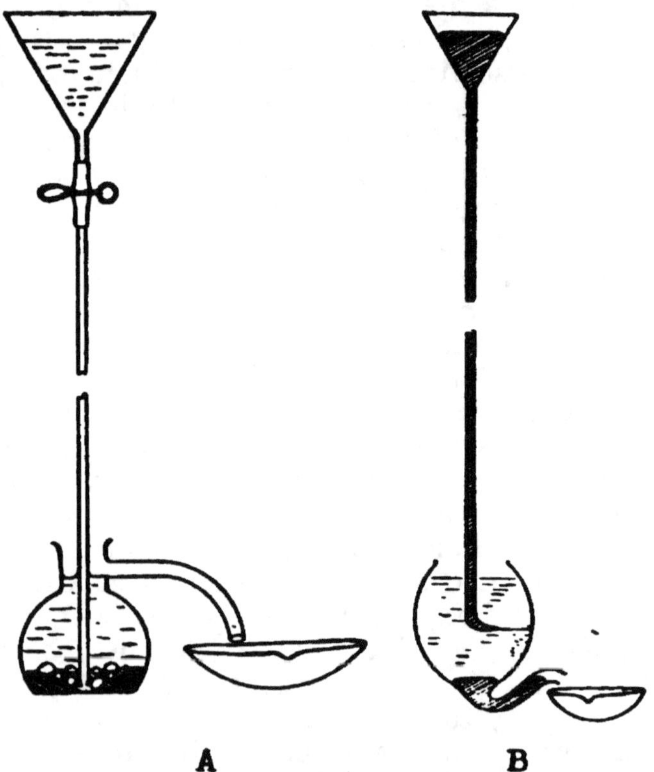

FIG. 21.—Two different methods of dispersing mercury.
(According to Nordlund.)

Nordlund demonstrated this fact by the following experiments (Fig. 21) :—

In experiment " A," water (mixed with potassium citrate to a concentration of $2 \cdot 5 \cdot 10^{-3}$ normal, in order to preserve the primary degree of dispersion and prevent coagulation) in the form of bubbles is forced to rise through mercury, producing very thin mercury lamellæ when reaching the surface of the mercury ; in experiment " B," mercury is ejected through a fine glass tube against a glass wall under water (mixed with potassium citrate as above).   In the former case a comparatively rich and very highly disperse mercury hydrosol is obtained ; in the latter, only a very dilute and coarsely disperse hydrosol.   Thus, by the bursting of the mercury lamellæ, a highly disperse system is obtained ; on the other hand, by breaking up mercury drops against a wall, only a slightly disperse system results.   The ultra-microscopic test showed that the particles were amicroscopic (with arc-light illumination and with a "slit ultra-microscope ") and smaller than the particles in any mercury sol yet known.   The author has carried out Nord-lund's experiments with the system oil-water, and found that in this case no clear difference appears between " A " and " B," very likely because of the low surface tension of the oil compared with mercury.

In the case of oils and fats, and when dealing with substances with low surface tension in general, rather highly disperse systems are obtained by the disruption of drops.   Thus, if a coarse fat emulsion is ejected against a hard wall, the fat droplets are disintegrated and, accordingly, the degree of dispersion is increased.   The so-called homogenization of milk is carried out in this manner (132).   Hot milk is forced between iron plates at a pressure of about 200 atmospheres ; a reduction of the size of the fat drops to about one-tenth is attained. When fats or hydrocarbons are emulsified with water, a little alkali (in the case of glycerides) or soap is usually added, in order to lower the surface tension (or interfacial tension) of the dispersion medium, thus facilitating the disintegration of the drops and preventing the small droplets formed from uniting again (133).

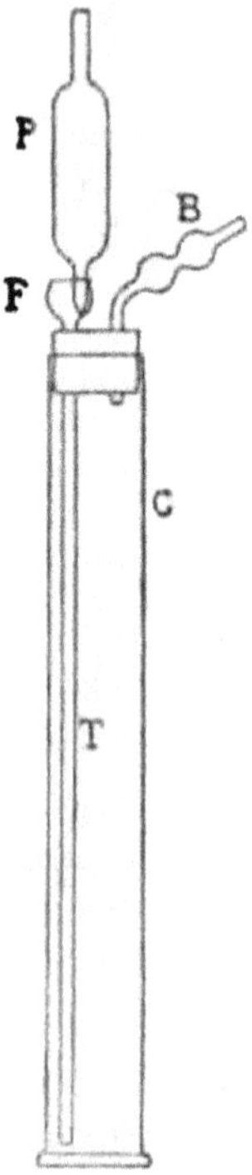

Hatschek, who has carried out a series of valuable investigations on emulsions (134), has given many good hints concerning the preparation of emulsions by mechanical dispersion. An automatic emulsifying apparatus devised by Hatschek is shown in Fig. 22 (135). The cylinder C is filled to about one-third with a suitable soap solution, *e.g.*, 1 per cent. sodium oleate, the oil to be emulsified is allowed to flow very slowly down from the pipette P through the funnel F and tube T, while the ball-tube B is connected to a filter pump. Provided the flow of oil be slow enough, the oil will form but a thin film on the inner wall of the tube T, and the air passing out at the lower edge of the tube will break it up into fine droplets. The air current at the same time causes a continuous thorough stirring, thus permitting the emulsification to go on automatically throughout the whole liquid. The percentage of disperse phase may rise to 70 or over.

FIG. 22.—Apparatus for the emulsifying of oils and hydrocarbons. (According to Hatschek.)

BIBLIOGRAPHY.

1. v. Weimarn, *Dispersoidchemie*, Dresden, p. 70 (1911).

2. Wo. Ostwald and v. Weimarn, *Koll. Zeitschr*, 6, 181 (1910).

3. Svedberg, English Patent No. 12108 (1908).

4. v. Weimarn, *Dispersoidchemie*, p. 67.

5. Reed, *Journ. Franklin Inst.*, **139**, 283 (1895). Haber, *Zeitschr. anorg. Chem.*, **16**, 438 (1898). Bredig and Haber, *Ber. deutsch. chem. Ges.*, **31**, 2741 (1898). Haber, *Zeitschr. Elektrochem.*, **6**, 40 (1900) ; **8**, 245 (1902) ; **11**, 660 and 828 (1905).

6. Malfitano, *Comptes rend.*, **139**, 1221 (1904). Bechhold, *Zeitschr. phys. Chem.*, **60**, 257 (1907) ; **64**, 328 (1908).

7. Graham, *Phil. Trans.*, **151**, 199 (1861).

8. See, *e.g.*, Odén, *Nova acta*, Upsala (4), **3**, No. 4, p. 66 (1913).

9. Jordis, *Zeitschr. Elektrochem.*, **8**, 677 (1902). Zsigmondy and Heyer, *Zeitschr. anorg. Chem.*, **68**, 169 (1910). Glenny and Walpole, *Biochem. Journ.*, **9**, 284 and 298 (1915). Wegelin, *Koll. Zeitschr.*, **18**, 225 (1916). Hatschek, *Laboratory Manual*, p. 16.

10. E. Fischer, *Ber. Deutsch. chem. Ges.*, **39**, 530 (1906).

10a. See Zsigmondy, *Kolloidchemie*, p. 315 (1918).

11. See Zsigmondy, *Kolloidchemie*, p. 307 (1918).

12. *Cf.* Svedberg, *Herstellung kolloider Lösungen*, p. 222.

13. Stoeckl and Vanino, *Zeitschr. phys. Chem.*, **30**, 98 (1899).

14. Nordenson, *Ueber die Bedeutung des Lichtes für die Bildung und Stabilität kolloider Lösungen*, Diss., Upsala, p. 107 (1914).

15. Reitstötter, *Kolloidchem. Beih.*, **9**, 248 (1917). Zsigmondy, *Kolloidchemie*, p. 148 (1918).

16. Doerinckel, *Zeitschr. anorg. Chem.*, **63**, 344 (1909). Westgren, *Die Brownsche Bewegung*, Diss., Upsala, p. 68 (1915).

17. Börjeson, *Koll. Zeitschr.*, **27**, 18 (1920).

18. Naumoff, *Zeitschr. anorg. Chem.*, **88**, 43 (1914).

19. Vanino and Hartl, *Koll. Zeitschr.*, **1**, 272 (1907).

20. Nordenson, Diss., *loc. cit.*, p. 114.

21. Zsigmondy, *Kolloidchemie*, p. 143 (1918).

22. Hiege, *Zeitschr. anorg. Chem.*, **91**, 145 (1915).

23. Gutbier, *Zeitschr. anorg. Chem.*, **31**, 448 (1902).

24. Svedberg, *Koll. Zeitschr.*, **5**, 318 (1909).

25. Nordenson, Diss., *loc. cit.*, p. 122.

26. Faraday, *Phil. Trans.*, **147**, 159 (1857).

27. Zsigmondy, *Zur Erkenntnis der Kolloide*, p. 100 (1905).

28. Zsigmondy, *Zur Erkenntnis der Kolloide*, pp. 136 and 173 (1905). Svedberg, *Koll. Zeitschr.*, **4**, 168 (1909) ; *Die Existens der Moleküle*, p. 10 (1912). Biltz, *loc. cit.*

29. Zsigmondy, *Zur Erkenntnis der Kolloide*, p. 128 (1905).

30. Siedentopf and Zsigmondy, *Annal. Phys.* (4), **10**, 1 (1903).

31. Tammann, *Zeitschr. phys. Chem.*, **25**, 441 (1898) ; *Zeitschr. Elektroch.*, **10**, 532 (1904).

32. See, *e.g.*, Vanino, *Zeitschr. prakt. Chem.* (2), **73**, 575 (1906). Svedberg, *Herstellung kolloider Lösungen*, p. 14 (1909). Wi. Ostwald, *Koll. Zeitschr.*, **4**, 5 (1909).

33. See abstract in *Annal. de Chim.*, **26**, 58 (1798).

34. Oberkampf, *Annal. de Chim.*, **80**, 140 (1811).

35. Faraday, *Phil. Trans.*, **147**, 145 (1857).

36. Kohlschütter, *Zeitschr. Elektroch.*, **14**, 49 (1908) ; *Koll. Zeitschr.*, **12**, 285 (1913).

37. Kohlschütter and Fischmann, *Liebigs Annal.*, **387**, 86 (1911).

38. Zsigmondy and Lottermoser, *Zeitschr. phys. Chem.*, **56**, 77 (1906).

39. Lüppo-Cramer, *Koll.-Zeitschr.*, **7**, 99 (1910).

40. Ca Lea, *Amer. Journ. Science* (3), **37**, 476 (1889). rey

41. Odén, *Zeitschr. phys. Chem.*, **78**, 682 (1912).

42. Kohlschütter, *Koll. Zeitschr.*, **12**, 289 (1913).

43. Billiter, *Ber. Deutsch. chem. Ges.*, **35**, 1929 (1902).

44. Blake, *Amer. Journ. Science* (4), **16**, 431 (1903).

45. Nordenson, *Kolloidchem. Beih.*, **7**, 130 (1915).

46. Svedberg, *Koll. Zeitschr.*, **6**, 129 (1910).

47. Traube-Mengarini and Scala, *Koll. Zeitschr.*, **6**, 65 and 240 (1910) ; **10**, 113 (1912).

48. Nordenson, *Kolloidchem. Beih.*, **7**, 91 (1915).

49. Svedberg, *Herstellung kolloider Lösungen*, p. 13 (1909).

50. Fulhame, *loc. cit.*

51. Oberkampf, *loc. cit.*

52. Vanino, *Ber. Deutsch. chem. Ges.*, **38**, 463 (1905).

53. Kohlschütter, *Zeitschr. Elektrochem.*, **14**, 49 (1908).

54. Zsigmondy, *Liebigs Annal.*, **301**, 29 (1898).

55. Fischer, *Annal. Phys.* (2), **9**, 255 (1827).

56. Lottermoser, *Journ. prakt. Chem.* (2), **57**, 484 (1898).

57. Billiter, *loc. cit.*

58. Gutbier, *Zeitschr. anorg. Chem.*, **32**, 51, 91, 106 and 347 (1902) ; **42**, 177 (1904). Gutbier and Hofmeier, *Journ. prakt. Chem.* (2), **71**, 358 and 452 (1905).

59. Paal, *Ber. Deutsch. chem. Ges.*, **35**, 2224 and 2236 (1902) ; **37**, 124 (1904) ; **38**, 526 and 534 and 1398 (1905) ; **39**, 1550 (1906) ; **40**, 1392 (1907) ; **50**, 722 (1917).

60. Rose, *Annal. Phys. u. Chem.* (2), **14**, 183 (1828).

61. Döbereiner, *Ann. Pharm.*, **2**, 4 (1832).

62. Wöhler, *Annal. Phys.* (2), **46**, 629 (1839).

63. Newbury, *Chem. News*, **54**, 57 (1886).

64. Muthmann, *Ber. Deutsch. chem. Ges.*, **20**, 983 (1887).

65. Selmi, *Annali del Majocchi*, **15**, 88, 212 and 235 (1844) ; *Ann. Chim. et phys.* (3), **28**, 210 (1850).

66. Engel, *Compt. rend.*, **112**, 866 (1891).

67. Raffo, *Koll. Zeitschr.*, **2**, 358 (1908).

68. Odén, *Nova acta*, Upsala (4), **3**, No. 4 (1913).

69. Wackenroder, *Arch. d. Pharm.*, 47, 272 (1846) ; 48, 140 (1846).

70. Selmi, *loc. cit.*.

71. Debus, *Journ. Chem. Soc.*, 53, 278 (1888).

72. Spring, *Rec. des trav. chim. des Pays-Bas*, 25, 253 (1906).

73. Lewes, *Journ. Chem. Soc.*, 41, 300 (1882).

74. Shaw, *Journ. Chem. Soc.*, 43, 351 (1883).

75. Hertlein, *Zeitschr. phys. chem.*, 19, 287 (1896).

76. Müller, *Zeitschr. Elektrochem.*, 11, 521 and 931 (1905) ; *Ber. Deutsch. chem. Ges.*, 38, 3779 (1905).

77. Scheele, *Efterlemnade bref och anteckningar utg. af Nordenskiöld*, Stockholm, pp. 416 and 448 (1892).

78. Bergman, *Kleine Physische und Chemische Werke*, Frankfurt am Mayn, 1, 342 (1782).

79. Le Veillard, *Crell's Chem. Annal.*, 1, 440 (1789).

80. Berthollet, *Annal. Chim.*, 25, 233 (1798).

81. Berzelius, *Lärobok i kemien*, Stockholm, 1, 120 (1808).

82. Döbereiner, *Schweiggers Journ.*, 8, 400 (1813).

83. Wackenroder, *loc. cit.*

84. Selmi, *loc. cit.*

85. Debus, *loc. cit.*

86. Wa. Ostwald, *Koll. Zeitschr.*, 15, 204 (1914).

87. See Acheson *Journ. Franklin Inst.*, 164, 375 (1907).   Thorne, *Journ. Chem. Soc.*, 109, 202 (1916).

88. R. Lorenz, *Zeitschr. anorg. Chem.*, 91, 46, 57 and 61 (1915) ; *Koll. Zeitschr.*, 18, 177 (1916).

89. Siedentopf, *Phys. Zeitschr.*, 6, 855 (1905).

90. Doelter, *Radium und die Farben*, Dresden (1910).

91. v. Weimarn, *Zur Lehre von den Zuständen der Materie*, p. 164 (1914).

92. Odén, *Arkiv för kemi*, Stockholm, 7, No. 26 (1920).

93. Berzelius, *Lehrb. der Chem.*, 5 Aufl., 2, 269 (1844).

94. Schulze, *Journ. prakt. Chem.* (2), 25, 431 (1882).

95. Picton and Linder, *Journ. Chem. Soc.*, 61, 137 (1892) ; 67, 63 (1895).

96. Svedberg, *Die Existenz der Moleküle*, p. 27 (1912).

97. Börjeson, *Koll. Zeitschr.*, 27, 18 (1920).

98. Linder and Picton, *Journ. Chem. Soc.*, 61, 114 (1892).

99. Lottermoser, *Journ. prakt. Chem.* (2), 75, 293 (1907).

100. Berzelius, *Lehrbuch der Chem.*, 3 Aufl., 3, 209 (1834).

101. Schulze, *Journ. prakt. Chem.* (2), 27, 320 (1883).

102. Winssinger, *Bull. Acad. Belg.* (3), 15, 390 (1888).

103. Paal and Voss, *Ber. Deutsch. chem. Ges.*, 37, 3862 (1904).

104. Berzelius, *Lehrb. der Chem.*, 3 Aufl., 3, 126, 209, 222 and 439 (1834).

105. Spring, *Chem. News*, 48, 101 (1883).

106. Goodwin, *Zeitschr. phys. Chem.*, 21, 1 (1896).

107. Svedberg, *Die Existenz der Moleküle*, p. 24.

108. Biltz, *Nachr. Ges. Wiss.*, Göttingen, Math.-Phys. Kl., 1906, p. 141.

109. Gay-Lussac, *Annal. de Chim.* 74, 193 (1810).

110. Berzelius, *Lehrb. der Chemie*, 3 Aufl., 2, 122 (1833).

111. Crum, *Journ. Chem. Soc.*, 6, 217 (1853).

112. Péan de Saint-Gilles, *Compt. rend.*, 40, 568 (1855).

113. Graham, *Phil. Trans.*, 151, 183 (1861).

114. Grimaux, *Compt. rend.*, 98, 105 and 1434 (1884).

115. Lottermoser, *Journ. prakt. Chem.* (2), 72, 39 (1905) ; 73, 374 (1906).

116. Zsigmondy, *Kolloidchemie*, p. 300 (1918).

117. Paal and Kühn, *Ber. Deutsch. chem. Ges.*, 39, 2859, 2863 (1906) ; 41, 51, 58 (1908).

118. Michael, *Ber. Deutsch. chem. Ges.*, **38**, 3217 (1905).

119. v. Weimarn, *Dispersoidchemie*, pp. 69 and 77 (1911).

120. Berzelius, *Annal. Phys.* (2), **32**, 1 (1834).

121. v. Weimarn, *Dispersoidchemie*, p. 79.

122. Wedekind, *Zeitschr. Elektrochem.*, **9**, 630 (1903).

123. Kužel, Österreich. Patent, Kl. 12*b*, No. A 2573 (1906).   Lottermoser, *Koll. Zeitschr.*, **2**, 347 (1908).

124. Davy, *Phil. Trans.*, 1809, p. 78.

125. Berzelius, *Vetenskapsacad. Handl.*, Stockholm, 1824, p. 89.

126. v. Weimarn, *Dispersoidchemie*, p. 82.

127. Pihlblad, *Lichtabsorption und Teilchengrösse*, Diss., Upsala, p. 46 (1918).

128. v. Weimarn, *Zur Lehre von den Zuständen der Materie*, p. 183 (1914).

129. Wegelin, *Koll. Zeitschr.*, **14**, 65 (1914).

130. See Bancroft, *Brit. Assoc. Report*, Sect. B, p. 6 (1918).

131. Nordlund, *Quecksilberhydrosole*, Diss., Upsala, p. 18 (1918) ; *Koll. Zeitschr.*, **26**, 121 (1920).

132. G. Buglia, *Koll. Zeitschr.*, **2**, 353 (1908). B. Spear, in Zsigmondy's *Chemistry of Colloids*, p. 265.

133. Donnan, *Zeitschr. phys. Chem.*, **31**, 42 (1899). Pickering, *Koll. Zeitschr..*, **7**, 11 (1910). Schlaepfer, *Journ. Chem. Soc.*, **113**, 522 (1918).

134. See, *e.g.*, *Brit. Assoc. Report* (1918).

135. Hatschek, *Laboratory Manual*, p. 63 (1920).

NAME INDEX.

Acheson, 91, 118
Andrén, 47, 53

Bancroft, 120
Barus, 53
Bechhold, 115
Benedicks, 34, 52
Bergman, 89, 118
Berthollet, 89, 118
Berzelius, 9, 13, 89, 101, 103, 105, 108, 110, 118, 119, 120
Billiter, 80, 82, 116, 117
Biltz, 14, 105, 116, 119
Blake, 80, 117
Börjeson, 30, 33, 37, 52, 63, 64, 102, 115, 119
Bredig, 24, 25, 52, 115
Buglia, 120
Bunsen, 92
Burton, 25, 52

Carey Lea, 79, 83, 116
Crum, 105, 119

Davy, 110, 120
Debus, 85, 90, 118
Degen, 25, 52
Döbereiner, 84, 89, 117, 118
Doelter, 93, 118
Doerinckel, 83, 115
Donnan, 120

Ehlers, 51
Ehrenhaft, 22, 42, 51
Engel, 84, 117

Faraday, 9, 14, 41, 52, 71, 75, 76, 83, 92, 116
Fischer, 82, 117
Fischer, E., 59, 115

Fischmann, 116
Fulhame, 75, 82, 117

Gay-Lussac, 105, 119
Glenny, 115
Goodwin, 104, 119
Graham, 9, 10, 13, 59, 90, 105, 106, 115, 119
Grimaux, 105, 119
Gutbier, 83, 116, 117

Haber, 56, 115
Hamburger, 15, 16, 18, 19, 21
Hartl, 115
Hatschek, 114, 115, 120
Hertlein, 85, 118
Heyer, 115
Hiege, 67, 69, 116
Hofmeier, 117
Houllevigue, 18

Jordis, 115
Juncher, 75

Kasperowicz, 53
Kimura, 21, 51
Knudsen, 15, 18
Kohlschütter, 14, 19, 20, 21, 30, 51, 53, 77, 78, 79, 82, 83, 116, 117
Konstantinowsky, 52
Kühn, 119
Kužel, 108, 109, 120

Lacroix, 53
Lemery, 75
Lenard, 47, 53
Le Veillard, 89, 118
Lewes, 85, 118
Lidow, 52

SUBJECT-MATTER INDEX.